Ailiya

The Lost
Sasquatch

Valerie Farr

This novel is a work of fiction. Names, characters, places and incidents are either the product of the author's imagination, or are used fictitiously. Any resemblance to actual person, living or dead, businesses, companies, events or locals is entirely coincidental.

ISBN: 978-0-9912646-0-5

Dedication

This book is dedicated to my Aunt, Judy Jones, and to the father of my children, Kevin Heaton. Both loved this story and encouraged me to write. Neither lived long enough to see it published.

Acknowledgements

I would like to acknowledge my parents, Jerry and Charlotte Farr, who raised me to enjoy nature, art, history, and to appreciate other cultures. We traveled throughout the Southwest, learning about past and present cultures as they taught me to see the beauty in everything.

I would also like to acknowledge my children, Justin and Emilse Heaton, who traveled to various sites with me in search of research and inspiration while I wrote this story (whether they wanted to or not!)

CONTENTS

Chapter 1

She had been seen! Ailiya thrashed through the bushes, heedless of the tufts of hair that were being caught on the sharp thorns. She only knew she must reach the cliff that dropped into Frye Canyon. Once she reached the safety of the canyon, she would be safe.

It had been curiosity that had drawn her from her cave. She had felt a great pain in the Earth, from the area north of her canyon home. Through the seasons, she had learned that this particular pain was caused by men. In the days before the noisy, fast creatures that belted smoke and fumes had invaded her world, this pain had been caused by men placing sticks in the ground and lighting strings that came from the sticks. As the flame touched the stick, the land was torn asunder, announcing the pain caused by the explosion with a roaring sound. The men would then use horses and wagons to remove the rubble that remained. They would take the rocks containing the warm, sun-colored metal called "gold" and the shiny-colored metal called "silver" in the language used by these men. Later they mined the black rock that burned with large machines and even larger explosions.

It had been many seasons since those days. The men and the creatures they used to move the rocks had changed quickly. They no longer relied upon the animals…the horse, the oxen or the mule. They built hard rock strips to travel from settlement to settlement. There were strange creatures in the sky that left long white tails in their passing. There was also so much noise! The first few times Ailiya felt the Earth's pain and had sought the cause, she felt much sadness as she saw the ground shattering, and she had stopped going to the areas where this was happening. She was the last of her people, and the onslaught of her native lands pushed her farther away from the mountain peaks she so loved.

She reached the cliff edge and threw herself out over the canyon, landing in the tops of the tall pines that stretched toward the sun. Once she was in the canyon, her breath slowed and she had reason to regret the way she had rushed away from the new wound that had been blown into the Earth. Her skin stung from the many places where her hair had been torn from her pelt. She wiped the tears away from her eyes, not knowing if they came from the pain caused to the Earth, of the shame in being seen or from the speed of her retreat into her peaceful, calm canyon.

Pausing, Ailiya heard the high screech of Ona, her favorite hawk. Listening to him as he descended to rest on her shoulder, she knew that while she had been seen, she had not been followed. She fed Ona a treat from one of the pockets in her vest. She saw some of the long hairs from the buffalo hide had also been torn loose in her careless flight. She sighed. There were very few buffalo hides remaining, hidden in the very back of her main cave, and those animals had long ago disappeared from the area. The pelts from the buffalo and the bear were the closest in length to her own hair. Her grandfather had told her stories from when he and others of their kind would release the buffalo and the mighty mammoth when their time had come to return to the Earth.

Ailiya reached the cool waters of the creek that flowed at the base of the canyon walls. She paused in a small pond, letting the water soothe the ache in her feet. With her head bowed, she closed her eyes and calmed her breathing, seeking the peace of the forest. Ona chirped inquiringly. Ailiya smiled at him as he used his sharp beak to burrow through her hair, trying to discover what had upset her. She gave him another treat and calmly told him what she had seen and why she had rushed back to the safety of her canyon so quickly.

She reached up and soothed his feathers as she continued down the canyon and toward her cave. While she had many caves throughout the area, most were kept hidden from all but the smartest animals. This cave was the one she considered her home. It was halfway up the canyon walls, hidden from any prying eyes because of its location beneath a large outcropping of bedrock. She grew bushes and sharp plants at the base of each trail leading to the cave to protect it further from the progressively inquisitive men that had come to inhabit the area. With her long limbs, she easily stepped over the plants and made her way up the small trail. Her heartbeat had returned to normal and she was breathing easily as she ducked behind the brush growing in front of her cave opening. She loved these bushes. As it was spring, they were covered in flowers, infusing the stuffiness of her cave with their lovely scent.

Ailiya sat on the rock that she had placed near the opening. It was comfortable, draped with a woven mat that was filled with feathers of all kinds. Ona dropped off her shoulder, swooping to the tree root that had intruded into the cave many seasons ago and now formed a natural stand for him to observe the activities in the cave. Ailiya shrugged out of her buffalo vest, emptying the many pockets and placing their contents into the various bowls that were placed behind her on a stone shelf. Each seed, nut, herb and other item had its own bowl. Some had been formed from wood, others from stone, and still others — ones that Ailiya most treasured — had been woven for her by her adopted Grandmother Hummingbird.

The last item she removed was the stone

talisman Laughing Boy had carved for her. It was of hematite, a magnetic stone she and her mother had brought back from the Yucatan. Originally, Thaena had bound three stones that had been split from one large stone. They brought back two stones, leaving the third with the young male who had brought Thaena the stones. Laughing Boy had carved two talismans, one for Thaena and the other for himself, as he prepared to leave in search of a partner. Laughing Boy had carved them from the same stone and said blessings over the pair, linking them spiritually. Hers looked similar to the paintings that they had brought with them from their visit in Mexico. They had described the different characters to Laughing Boy and he had carved hers to be reminiscent of Tezcatlipoa as the ""Smoking Mirror"" or the "God of the Night" of the Mayan people who had inhabited the area. Many times Tezcatlipoa was shown with his right foot replaced with obsidian or with hematite. Sometimes he was shown with the mirror on his chest and four arrows in his right hand to punish the sins of man. That's how her carving appeared, but it also featured a turquoise bag in the god's left hand. Laughing Boy said that the bag contained healing powers to balance the sins of man with the hope of the future.

Holding her talisman, she rubbed her thumb over it. Just holding her talisman brought back memories of the days with Laughing Boy — days when her mother and grandfather were still with her. Several tears fell on the arrow side of the talisman. Sniffing, she wiped the tears away and placed the talisman in the bowl Laughing Boy's wife had woven from his hair.

* * *

She couldn't believe what she had just seen! Mariana double-checked the view screen of her digital Canon 60D camera. It was blurry, but she would work with her photo programs to bring more clarity to the scene. She had been sent to document the blasting for the new golf course and housing development south of Flagstaff, Arizona. She was a reporter who worked for the *Arizona Daily Sun*. She already had taken several good shots of the exploding Earth and had interviewed the developer and the construction management team. This was one of the largest and one of the most expensive developments in Flagstaff's history, which is why her editor had sent her to cover the "explosive" ground breaking. She had grumbled at what she had considered an inferior assignment. But now excitement filled her, and the sense that she was onto a story brought out her reporter's instincts. She hadn't felt like this since she had left Los Angeles.

She had only been working at the *Daily Sun* in Flagstaff for the past few months. She had originally worked in Los Angeles for the *Times*. She was used to covering drug stings and corrupt government employees. She had stumbled onto some volatile information on one of the mayor's assistants. When she had approached her editor with the possible story line, she was abruptly pulled off all of her assignments and given a leave of absence. She found that she was being systematically "blackballed" by the newspaper industry. She started calling some of her old contacts, and they suggested that she might need to leave the state. She had managed to upset some very high-powered individuals who had put pressure on other newspapers, not only throughout the state but also in other major cities in the west.

Mariana had packed her bags and had started driving east. When she reached Flagstaff, she was thrilled with the scenery and with the thought of snow in what she considered "the desert." She had gone into the offices of the *Daily Sun*, Flagstaff's newspaper. She met the managing editor before lunch and had asked to take him out. During lunch, she frankly described the position in which she had found herself in Los Angeles and had asked to be taken on as a free-lance reporter. Frank Donaldson appraised the young woman. Mariana had black hair and intense blue eyes that expressed her inner strength and determination. Her openness in approaching him, along with her honesty, convinced Frank to bring her on board full time as a reporter, instead of merely free-lance. Frank warned her that she would end up starting from the bottom until she proved herself.

After hiring her, Frank had actually heard the rumors concerning the troubles that Mariana had been going through, but had gone through back issues containing her articles and had liked the way she approached stories. He had also worked in Los Angeles, free-lancing for several newspapers and was tired of the city rat race. He loved to hike, bike and camp. Spending hours in traffic every day seemed to suck the life out of him. He had met his wife while biking, and she had threatened to leave him if they didn't leave the city. They had decided to settle in Flagstaff, Arizona, where Amy, his wife, had spent her summers. Through working several jobs and free-lancing, they eventually were able to build a home out in Baderville, and Frank worked his way up through the newspaper ranks until he became the managing editor. Amy was an artist, who had become a fixture in the downtown art scene.

Mariana's intensity reminded Frank of himself when he had fled the city and started a new life. He knew that while Mariana might have a difficult time adjusting to the slower pace of the relatively sleepy town of Flagstaff, he felt that she would be good for the staff at the *Sun*. They shook hands, and Frank gave her the name and phone number of a friend who might have a room for rent. When Frank told Amy about Mariana, she had him invite her over for dinner. After that, they adopted Mariana as part of their family, including her as a guest at frequent barbecues and introducing her to mountain biking and camping. While she wasn't as comfortable with the outdoors, she was learning to enjoy the peacefulness of the surrounding forest. She was finding it difficult to adjust to a slower pace of life, and part of her still yearned for more excitement.

Chapter 2

Dr. Morgan Nezhoni was in the middle of his guest lecture at Northern Arizona University. A structural engineer, Morgan had received his bachelor's degree in civil engineering at NAU and had gone on to get his master's and doctorate degrees in Tucson, from the University of Arizona. Peggy Alvarez, a former undergraduate student of his, now taught at NAU and had asked Morgan to give a lecture on the archaeology dig in which he had participated in conjunction with UA. They had been excavating archaeology sites in the Yucatan. Morgan had been a part of the team because of the stone structures they had been excavating. He was charged with verifying the stability of the structures and temporary shoring as needed. In addition, both of his parents worked with the dig, his mother as an archaeologist and his father as an anthropologist.

His PowerPoint presentation included a variety of photos of the structures they had unearthed and how his engineering background was also used in determining how many people would have lived in the city. Underground water storage areas had been uncovered, and the potential volume of these storage areas could be used to calculate the number of people who had lived in the city. He was showing the fascinating hydrologic systems used to transport the water from several cenotes when he felt a powerful pain in the middle of his chest. He paused, catching his breath, and the pain repeated. He flipped to the next slide and let the students and faculty review the technical information from the dig. He reached to his chest and found his stone talisman to be at the location of the pain. He grabbed the leather straps and pulled the talisman over his head, holding it in one hand. The pain was now emanating from his hand, but he was able to talk through it.

He concluded his presentation and asked for questions. The students were typically in their first or second years of engineering study. Peggy taught an introduction to engineering course, which gave overviews of the multiple disciplines within the field of engineering. Many of the students were surprised that an engineer would participate in archaeology. Morgan discussed a presentation he had heard when he was at NAU as a student. His professor had worked with an archaeology dig in Egypt, and his skills were utilized in a similar manner as his had been in the Yucatan. They had uncovered a sectional clay pipe that had transported water to a Roman fort. Morgan's professor had been able to estimate not only the number of men who would have been stationed at the fort, but also the number of animals and horses that would have supported the men in the desert heat. In evaluating the storage areas, the size of the pipe and with the slope and distance from the water source, he was able to calculate the amount of water which would have been available.

By this time, the pain from the talisman was coming in sharper bursts. He dropped the talisman out of his hand, holding on to the straps only. This only brought a warm, pulsing sensation to his hand. The lights were turned on and Morgan wrapped up his presentation, referring students to his website for further information. He packed up his papers and reference material as Peggy concluded her class and the bells rang. The students rushed off to their next class, along with the faculty members who had sat in for Morgan's lecture. Several of them had been his own teachers ten years ago, when he was an undergrad. He told Peggy that he wasn't feeling well and declined the lunch that they had planned. She looked concerned and disappointed, but could see that he was experiencing some type of discomfort.

Morgan found himself sitting in his Jeep, gazing at the talisman, which he had hung from his rearview mirror. He was trying to figure out what was going on. As an engineer, he considered himself to be a scientist, and this definitely didn't make scientific sense. He knew that he had received the talisman when he was young, and that he had always worn it. Although he had a strong Native American background, his parents were not "traditional" and were from separate tribes. They had both been archaeologists and had traveled around the world, taking Morgan with them. He remembered staying on the Navajo Indian Reservation when he was seven, while his parents had gone to a dig in a dangerous area of South America.

In his geology class, he had learned that his talisman had been formed from a magnetic mineral, hematite. It was not one of the typical talisman shapes common to the Navajo and Hopi traditions of his father. His mother's ancestry was Apache and Hispanic, but he didn't find anything similar in those traditions, either. It appeared to be a maiden, with incised hair down to her feet. Turquoise and shell were inlaid on the front of the maiden, showing her to be holding corn. Morgan had never been able to find another talisman that was anything similar to his. During his archaeological dig, one of the students had seen it one day when he removed his shirt because of the extreme humidity. The student, Mary Angelo, said it seemed to be a representation of Xilonen. The Mayans believed her to be the goddess of young maize. She was the wife of Tezcatlipoa, and she was called the "Hairy One" for the tassels of the corn. Mary went on to describe Tezcatlipoa as the ""Smoking Mirror"" or the "God of the Night". Many times Tezcatlipoa was shown with his right foot replaced with obsidian or with hematite. Sometimes he was shown with the mirror on his chest and four arrows in his right hand to punish the sins of man. Mary was quite interested in his talisman and wanted to show their professor, who was in charge of the dig. Morgan declined. He was uncomfortable with others paying attention to his talisman, even though he did not follow the traditions of his father's people.

He now felt that the talisman was somehow tied to a dream he had as a young child and that there was significance in the pain he had felt. He reached up and held the stone in his hand. Instead of pain, he felt a pull, from deep within himself. He put the leather thongs back over his head and the pull felt even greater. He put his Jeep into gear and started driving.

Chapter 3

Her thoughts took her back to when she had discovered Grandmother Hummingbird. The air had been much cleaner and crisper then. The Earth shook around the great mountain peaks. And at times, rock spewed from the smaller pointed hills with great fire and smoke. During those times, Ailiya and her family lived farther south, gathering the special herbs and plants from the dry lands. There were still visits by others of their kind, the Elo-ai-ne. Not as many, but enough to bring news from the great settlements in the northwest. Ailiya's family had been chosen for its stability. They didn't have the wanderlust that seemed to grip so many of their kind. It was their task to establish a way-station of sorts, a place of safety where those who were traveling would find a warm meal, a soft bed and news of other outposts. Theirs, particularly, was a choice location for travel in any direction as it was an intersection for East and West travel, as well as the start of the trail to the southern lands.

In those seasons, the peoples of the land thought that Ailiya and her family were animal spirits, and they kept their distance. The people also feared and revered the mountains that spewed fire and thought of them as homes to other spirits. Ailiya's family discovered the dark-haired people of the area would leave them offerings of animals, woven objects and other gifts. Ailiya's kind had respect for all beings and accepted these gifts and kept to themselves, not intruding upon the lives of the people in the land, unless they were called upon to warn them of impending danger.

One day, Ailiya had been gathering flowers for a garland she was making for her mother. She was young, but tall for her age. At the base of the great mountain was her favorite location for flowers. Where the water sprung from the rock, she would find many colorful fields of flowers. She had already made a small garland for herself and had almost finished the garland for her mother. There was a buzzing in the air, made by the multiple insects also enjoying the fragrant fields. Over the buzzing, Ailiya heard a different sound, a moaning, a sound of pain. She placed the garlands and the flowers into the woven grass bag that she carried over her back. Standing up, she caught a whiff of a scent she hadn't smelled before. It wasn't pleasant and it made her feel uncomfortable. Again she heard the moaning sound and followed it to a small female of the people, collapsed on the ground. Her eyes were closed, and there was an arrow shaft protruding from her shoulder. Blood had soaked the clothing the woman wore.

Ailiya had never been this close to a person of the land. She had seen the hunting groups and the women and children from a distance. Her parents had insisted that she not approach them, saying that their kind made them feel uncomfortable. She edged closer to the woman on the ground, who had opened her eyes when she heard Ailiya move through the tall grass. She had wrinkly skin and gray hair that only covered her head. She did not appear to be afraid of Ailiya and muttered some words that Ailiya didn't understand, as her eyes closed again. Ailiya knelt next to the old woman and placed her hand upon the woman's head. She could feel the physical pain that the woman was feeling, and she gasped as she also understood the mental and emotional pain that the woman was experiencing.

It was a special gift that Ailiya and those like her had been given by the Great One. They could touch a rock, a plant, a tree or another being and sense pain, sadness or other great emotion. The more complex the object or being, the more detail they could sense. In this instance, Ailiya could see flashes of what she didn't completely understand but, after concentrating harder, was able to piece together that this woman's family had been attacked by a neighboring tribe. Through the flashes, Ailiya saw this woman grabbing a baby from a pile of skins and turning to run. She felt the searing pain as the arrow had penetrated her shoulder; she fell to the ground, protecting the baby by curling around him. She had lain in this position until she could no longer hear the shrieks and cries from her family members. Once it had become dark, she had picked up the infant and struggled toward the sacred mountain, knowing that those who had attacked her would not venture near.

As Ailiya saw this, she immediately looked around, spying the bundle that mewed and wiggled next to the injured woman. She reached over, removing the wrapping and uncovering a round-faced infant with large brown eyes. The eyes looked up at Ailiya, and the infant smiled. She reached down and the infant grabbed her finger, pulling at the fine hairs that covered Ailiya's hand. The infant gurgled and laughed as Ailiya talked to him in the language of the Elo-ai-ne. Ailiya's language was very melodic, sounding at once like the wind through the trees, the rain on the lakes and the music of the Earth. Ailiya picked up the bundle of skins swaddling the infant and placed the infant in the woven bag on her back. She then turned to the old woman, carefully picking her up as she had seen mothers pick up their babies. Even as young as she was, she was taller than the old woman and very strong. The woman moaned but didn't open her eyes again.

Ailiya moved swiftly through the meadows and stands of trees, taking the woman and infant to one of the small storage caves that were close by. She placed the old woman on a pile of boughs that had been gathered to be woven into mats for visitors. She made a small pile of skins with a depression in the middle, where she deposited the gurgling infant. She smiled as the infant contentedly cooed, looking trustingly up at Ailiya. The old woman was still. The arrow appeared to have been jostled during the trip to the cave and was bleeding afresh. Ailiya took tinder and stone from her vest pocket and started a fire near the old woman, covering her with another of the stored skins. Checking that the baby couldn't turn over or accidentally fall into the flames, she left to fetch her mother.

* * *

"Ailiya! Slow down, tell me what happened." Her mother patiently brushed the long hairs over Ailiya's eyes back over her head. Ailiya had just rushed into one of the guest caves her mother was cleaning. She gulped air from her run through the forest, calming herself as her mother had taught her. She sought her center and the peace of the Earth beneath her feet. She slowed her thoughts and turned toward her mother. She explained who she had seen and what she had done. Her mother was able to understand and pick up flashes of what Ailiya had seen. As Ailiya was explaining, her mother took her hand, leading her to the healing cave, picking up one of the vests and putting various herbs and mixtures into different pockets. She handed soft skins and cattails to Ailiya, along with a cooking basket, which she filled with a special healing mix that would be cooked into a soup to feed the woman. Before leaving the cave, Thaena grabbed a bladder of water that had hung near the entry. She then had Ailiya guide her to the cave where she had left the old woman and the infant.

They could hear a high-pitched shriek as they neared the cave. Ailiya began to worry that she had placed the infant too close to the fire and rushed into the cave. To her relief, the infant was still safely bundled in the little nest that Ailiya had made. There were tears coursing down the round cheeks, and the small fists were closed and flailing widely. Since Ailiya had done all that she knew how to do for the old woman, she sat down away from the fire and began to unwrap the infant. Thaena saw that the infant was unharmed; the crying sound indicated that a change of wraps and a full stomach would settle it to sleep, and she turned her attention to the old woman.

The woman had been placed on her side so that the arrow wasn't touching the ground. Her eyes were still closed and it appeared as if the bleeding had stopped again. Thaena used a sharpened stone to cut the animal skin covering that the old woman was wearing. The arrow had entered her back; the tip was just protruding through the skin on the front of her shoulder. Thaena felt the woman's life force as she cleaned the wound, catching glimpses of what Ailiya had attempted to relay. Ailiya had never had cause to search for a person's life force before and had been confused at the images that the old woman had given to her. Once clean, she saw that the arrow shaft would need to be broken off near the old woman's back and the head with the remaining shaft pulled through the wound. This would be a very delicate healing requiring all of her senses, and she needed to center herself before attempting to help the woman.

Knowing that the woman was stable, Thaena now turned her attention to the infant. Ailiya had managed to unwrap the baby and console it so that it wasn't shrieking anymore, although it had begun hiccoughing between laughing at the faces and sounds that Ailiya was making. Thaena prepared a small bladder with water and a dried mixture to help nourish the infant until they could find a source of milk. "Look, Mom, it's a boy!" Ailiya used one of the skins to clean the baby as she had seen mothers do before wrapping him in a new skin, with the shredded material of the cattails used to catch any droppings of the baby boy. Thaena handed Ailiya the bladder and showed her how to carefully drip the mixture into the baby's mouth. The baby looked uncertainly at Ailiya, but swallowed the mixture and began to urgently suckle against the tightened opening of the bladder. Thaena cautioned her daughter to keep the baby from swallowing too much at one time as he could choke. She watched Ailiya for several moments until she was satisfied that the baby knew what to do and that Ailiya knew what to watch out for. She then turned her attention back to the old woman.

Hummingbird had heard the sounds coming from the great creatures and the contented sounds from her grandson as his needs were met. She had never had contact with the creatures called the "Hairy Ones." They had always accepted the gifts of her people and had not interfered with their activities. They had sent warnings when changes in the Earth were coming, and they helped the people know when to burn the plains to help their crops grow better. Hummingbird had sometimes seen their kind from a distance, their shadows moving swiftly across the landscape. In her fevered state, after the arrow had penetrated her body, she knew that she would head toward the sacred mountains and put herself and her grandson at the mercy of the large creatures.

She looked up now into kindly eyes. She didn't speak their language, but felt their intelligence in the way they spoke to each other and cared for Laughing Boy. She had thought the creature who found her had been large, but she could see that she must have been just a child because now a much larger creature bent over her. She reached up a shaky hand, grasping the fur-covered fingers of the large creature, feeling the strength and the gentleness. With a nod, she looked down at the arrow shaft, back up at the large hair-covered face and closed her eyes. She felt a strip of leather being gently pushed between her teeth. Thaena gently covered the top of the old woman's head with her hand, giving to her of her own life force and trying to give images to soothe the old woman.

Thaena prepared the materials needed to remove the arrow and to treat the wound. Breaking off the arrow shaft behind the old woman's back would cause her pain that was unavoidable. She braced the woman and broke the shaft cleanly off several inches above the woman's back. She felt the woman lose consciousness, grateful for this blessing as the next step would be even more painful. She cleaned the remaining shaft so that upon its removal, no further dirt or debris would be brought into the wound. This was not her first experience with removing arrows or other objects, but this was her first time to attempt to heal a native woman. Her experience had all been upon animals of the forest or the dry land and on other Elo-ai-ne. If their life force was strong and the wound not life-taking, she would remove the arrow and heal the animal, releasing it back to nature once it was sufficiently healed. If the animal knew that it was at the end of its life, she accepted its gift and made its passing swift. Her people did not eat animals. They ate the plants of the Earth. When an animal came to her to offer its life force, she kept the portions that they could use — the skin, the bones, the bladder and sinews. The meat and other portions were set out for the carnivorous animals and birds to use.

After removing the rest of the arrow shaft, she bathed the native woman's wound, packed it with various healing herbs and bound up both sides with separate skins. Thaena then checked the old woman over, finding no additional wounds besides various scrapes from her falls, cleaning these as she went. She made her comfortable upon the bed of boughs and skins, raising her head to feed her some of the same mixture that she had prepared for the baby, when she regained consciousness. The woman weakly allowed the mixture to drop down her throat, raising her hand to Thaena's when she could swallow no more. Thaena then laid the old woman's head onto extra skins and bathed her face with a cool skin. By this time, Ailiya had finished feeding the baby and had placed the infant on her shoulder and was gently patting his back, as she had seen other mothers do after their infants had fed. His eyes closed sleepily as a large burp escaped his lips, his head falling gently onto her shoulder. Thaena helped her lower the infant to his sleeping nest and cover him.

Thaena and Ailiya left the cave to join the others. Thaena left her bird, a beautiful, pearl-colored female hawk named Arot, at the entrance of the cave with instructions to come get her if she heard movements from the old woman or the infant. As they walked, Thaena softly praised Ailiya for her clear head and quick thinking. She told her that while the old woman's life force was weak, her spirit was strong. Thaena explained the images that Ailiya had seen but not understood, of the enemy of the old woman's people who had attacked their camp and killed all of her family except for herself and her grandson. Ailiya was able to understand these images now, with the help of her mother. She showed her mother the crushed garlands that she had made for them and Thaena took the one made for herself and placed it proudly on her head and told Ailiya that she was very happy that Ailiya cared more for someone's life force than for the gift for her mother.

It took the passing of many suns before Grandmother Hummingbird was able to care for herself and for Laughing Boy. Ailiya spent many happy hours caring for the two and trying to learn the language that Grandmother Hummingbird patiently spoke for her. Ailiya would bring the old woman various plants, rocks and feathers and ask her what they were or who they belonged to. When Ailiya was unable to understand the curious sounds that Grandmother Hummingbird made, she would gently touch her hand and an image was given to her mind. She would laugh and say what the object was in her own language. The language of the people was simple for her to understand. As Laughing Boy learned to sit up and make his own sounds, both Grandmother Hummingbird and Ailiya would teach him the words of their languages. Thaena often carried Laughing Boy with her as she would take her morning walk to greet the morning. They would stare toward the east, waiting for the morning sun to peek over the edge of the Earth. Every morning was met by laughter from Laughing Boy when he stared with delight as the first rays of the morning sun bathed the Earth. Grandmother Hummingbird had carried Laughing Boy to greet the day until he had become too heavy for her and she couldn't walk anymore. It was the tradition of The People to greet each day. Grandmother Hummingbird had described the importance to Thaena and it was Thaena who took the place of Grandmother Hummingbird each morning. As she carried Laughing Boy, she whispered stories of their kind and stories of The People. In this way, he grew until he could walk on his own, holding the fine, furred hand in his own.

* * *

The moon had come many times since Ailiya had found Grandmother Hummingbird and Laughing Boy. Thaena had explained to Grandmother Hummingbird that their kind rested during the cold moons. They did not sleep away the cold moons as do the bears, but it was similar. Thaena had gathered and stored up more food and fuel for the fires for which Grandmother Hummingbird and Laughing Boy would need for the coming moons while Thaena and Ailiya rested. Ailiya did not understand why they must go to the sleeping caves. She wanted to stay and play with Laughing Boy. He was trying to run and climb the rocks with her. She sulked until her mother reminded her that Laughing Boy slept every night; that he required this rest or he would be grumpy, just like she was now because it was time for her to rest. With tearful goodnights, Ailiya hugged Laughing Boy and Grandmother Hummingbird. Grandmother Hummingbird told her to sleep deeply and dream of flowered meadows.

As the last of the fall moon disappeared and the aspen leaves turned gold, then brown and dropped to the Earth, Grandfather, Thaena and Ailiya went to their sleeping cave, high on the mountain. Grandfather sealed the opening with large boulders to keep the snow and small animals from joining them and disturbing their rest. Thaena had placed soft pallets of bear skins on top of boughs gathered earlier. Upon a small stone shelf sat baskets, woven by Grandmother Hummingbird, filled with different nuts, seeds and roots. Due to their long-haired pelts, they didn't require exterior heat sources like Grandmother Hummingbird and Laughing Boy. The sleeping cave would be warm through the long cold moons. It had been formed by a lava flow, with a lava tube remaining and retaining the heat of their bodies. The three of them would sleep as needed, eat if they felt like it and drink from the spring that burbled quietly near the front of the cave.

At times during this period of rest, when Ailiya awoke, Grandfather would tell her stories of his parents and of the changes in the land. He didn't sleep as much as Ailiya and he spent much of the winter months carving their history on great ivory tusks. Thaena would write the history that had already been carved on the tusks onto folded sheets of paper that they had brought back from their trip to the southern lands. The people who had lived in the country had many books written in this manner. The paper, formed from the pulp of a tree, was pounded flat and then carefully folded. Thaena wanted to ensure that Ailiya would understand the written text as well as the carved text that

Grandfather was making. The history of the Elo-ai-ne had been collected and sealed in the Earth when they had the great convocation in Mexico. What Thaena was writing was the history of her own ancestors. Their numbers had dwindled, and many of their kind had become separated from others. Thaena was worried that Ailiya would not know of the richness of their traditions, and about their ancestors especially. The Elo-ai-ne did not have rulers or royalty, but Thaena's family had been the closest of their kind to the tradition of the peoples of the land. Their line included gifted seers, healers and watchers of the land.

Chapter 4

Ailiya awoke from her remembrances. She looked down at the delicate basket that Grandmother Hummingbird had woven for her from Ailiya's own hair. She laughed, for while her hair hadn't grown long, like Grandmother Hummingbird's gray hair or like Laughing Boy's before he left them in search of a mate, she had more of it than both of them put together! Inside the little basket, Grandmother Hummingbird had placed several special, sacred objects. She had shaped a bear talisman for Ailiya, weaving a long string that allowed her to wear the talisman if she wished. She included a dried hummingbird, her own namesake for Ailiya, reminding her that the hummingbirds could find water and plants in the dry lands. Other items were included that Grandmother Hummingbird told her she would learn about when the time was right and her own understanding was ready.

Ona chirped, asking Ailiya what was bothering her and making her laugh like a silly coyote. Ailiya stood, stretching muscles too little used to fast running anymore. She shook her head, feeling surprised at being caught after all of these seasons. Grandmother Hummingbird and Laughing Boy had gone to the Earth many seasons ago. The land had become dry, and all of the people had left the area around the sacred mountains. When Laughing Boy had reached manhood, Grandmother Hummingbird had directed him to where her family had always wintered. There had been tears and gifts when he had left them. They did not know if they would see him again. Grandmother Hummingbird's health deteriorated until she couldn't see anymore. Thaena had made one of the caves as comfortable as they could for her to weather all seasons. She would make bowls and cups and other utensils out of clay for them to use with the visitors. During the winter, she would weave baskets and sew new vests. Her fingers were so tiny and her stitches so fine, that Thaena left all of the sewing to her. It left her free to gather the foods and materials that Grandmother Hummingbird would need for the long winter moons.

Ailiya put down the basket, wondering at herself. She was surprised that she had felt such curiosity that she had deliberately wandered close to the sacred mountain where the rents in the Earth had occurred. Because the floor of her cave was part of the bedrock that sloped close to the surface of the Earth near the sacred mountain, she had felt the dull whumps of power before she felt the rending force. She had long been living her life at night, exploring the area and gathering the food and materials that she needed. She only ventured toward the Sacred Mountain as the time neared for her to journey to the sleeping cave. There were too many people and fast creatures that had begun to intrude upon her area. They even moved about at night now, the creatures with eyes that glowed brightly and lit up the night sky and the stone path they traveled upon.

She turned toward the back of the cave, straightening things as she went. She normally left her cave very tidy, but she had departed in such a heedless rush when she felt the Earth's pain through the floor of her cave. Ona, having no response to his prodding, flew out of the cave in search of his evening meal. Ailiya reached the rear of the cave, opposite her bed area. She lifted the top off the coarsely woven box and examined the three remaining vests that had been sewn by Grandmother Hummingbird and her descendants. She picked up the one on top. Laughing Boy had returned one spring day, with two children of his own and his pregnant wife Altua. She had been startled when she had been introduced to Grandfather, Thaena and Ailiya. Grandmother Hummingbird cried as she heard the mature voice of Laughing Boy trying to speak in Ailiya's language. She knew that she would not have survived the next cold moons with Thaena and Ailiya sleeping. Laughing Boy told her that he had a dream of a hummingbird zooming around the outside of the stone house he and Altua had built. The hummingbird had changed into a snowball and had rolled down the cliff, disappearing into the night. He told Altua about his "family" and told her of his dream. They had begun gathering their belongings and the supplies they would need to cross the dry lands to reach the sacred mountains. Her family had cried and gave them gifts for their travels.

The pale-skinned people who next came did not revere the mountain or Ailiya's kind. They did not leave gifts for them or respect the animals. Doba, one of the last of Laughing Boy's descendants, explained about the noisy creatures that moved along a metal ribbon. She said that they were called trains and that they carried many pale-skinned people across the country. The smaller vehicles were called horseless carriages as the horses no longer pulled wagons. Doba had brought many different types of beads and shells when she had returned to the land of the Sacred Mountain. She had sewn these beads, not on the outside of the long, hair-covered vests, but on the inside, next to Ailiya's heart. The vests were worn to help Ailiya carry the tools and supplies she needed away from the cave, but did not detract from her ability to blend into the mountain landscape.

Ailiya replaced the vest, disturbing the child's picture book that Doba had brought to her. Doba had been taken from the reservation, to a boarding school, and missionaries had brought books to them, teaching them their language, English. Ailiya lovingly caressed the worn pages, now yellowing and cracking. Ailiya had dutifully practiced the English letters and words that Doba had taught her. Her great grandmother Rozene knew that in the coming age, Ailiya would have to be even more careful and would have to learn to be a creature of the night in order to avoid detection. The origin of Doba's name was "No War." She had been born many years after her parents had returned from "The Long Walk" from Bosque Redondo.

Chapter 5

Morgan felt drawn toward the back roads to the southwest of Flagstaff. It had been many years since he had wandered around these dirt roads. He had usually been in pursuit of some new lake to fish in or camping with his friends. He used the back roads to escape from the pressures of attending school full time and working for one of his professors as a surveyor. There were times when he just had to leave concrete and asphalt behind, in search of something he had never quite been able to define.

As he drew closer to Frye Canyon, his talisman felt warmer. When he reached an area that was as close to the canyon as conventional roads allowed, he pulled off the dirt road and parked his Jeep. He pulled a bottle of water from behind his seat and changed into the hiking boots he kept in his vehicle. He checked his cell phone, but he had no service. He put it in one of his pockets anyway, just in case. He also picked up a small, hand-held radio that could broadcast on various channels. He did not know what he was getting into, and this was the best that he could do to prepare himself.

He studied the canyon, searching for a way down. He walked for about a mile, heading southeast at the top of the canyon, before he found a game trail that led down toward the bottom. As he climbed down into the canyon, he thought about the dream he had as a child — or at least what he always remembered as a dream. He had been left with his dad's sister's family on the Navajo Indian Reservation. It was winter, and as he was homeschooled, he had a lot of time to explore the surrounding area. It was several weeks before he noticed the old hogan back in one of the canyons. The family didn't mention anyone who lived nearby. It was a different experience living on the reservation. Neither of his parents was considered "traditional." In fact, both of them were in professions that were avoided by tribal members as they dealt with the dead. His parents were archaeologists and anthropologists. They felt that it was their duty to bring the past to life and to deal with the many misconceptions of history.

* * *

He had passed the old, crumbling hogan when he smelled tea. He turned toward the hogan and heard an old voice warble, "Ashkii!" He knew from his father that this meant "boy" in Navajo. While his parents had taught him both Apache and Navajo, neither were his first language and he had to work at translating. He was walking toward the deerskin that served as the door to the old hogan, when it was lifted up at one side by a cane. He again heard, "Ashkii!" He replied in English that he was coming. He entered the hogan, lifting the deerskin hide away, and pausing at the entrance to let his eyes adjust to the dim lighting. Sitting on a pile of rugs, to the right of the door, he saw a tiny, white-haired Navajo woman. There was a fire burning in the middle, with a metal teapot hanging from a tripod over the fire. She poked him with her cane and then looked down at the two chipped mugs placed upon an upturned milk crate that was sitting between her and the fire. He looked around and found a cloth that had obviously been used as a hot pad. He reached over, removed the teapot and with a glance at the woman, poured the tea into both cups. She nodded gravely and then indicated that he should sit. He looked around the inside of the hogan. The interior was like a time warp, from the last century. Old books were up on shelves, close by the old woman. There were bear skin rugs and deer hides in piles. Old tin cans lined shelves alongside what he knew were extremely valuable hair baskets and ceramic bowls. To his left was a large weaving loom with multiple colors of wool, wrapped for weaving. From the ceiling, he saw many plants hanging and in various stages of drying. The smoke escaped from the hogan through a hole at the top.

The old woman reached forward and grasped the mug nearest her and took a long sip. She glanced at him and then down at his mug, so he picked it up and took a sip. It was very good. He had never tasted anything like it. He looked at her and said, "I am Morgan". She took another sip, still looking at him. His parents had taught him the manners that were expected toward the Elders of the tribes, whether male or female. He took another sip and waited for her to tell him why he had been invited to enter the hogan.

She took another sip and then started looking at objects in the hogan or pointing towards them with her cane and looking back at Morgan. He would say the English name and then he would say the Navajo or Apache name if he remembered it. After going through most of the small room, she grunted and finished her tea. Morgan poured her another cup and she started indicating various items around her and giving him the proper Navajo and Apache name for each item. After she finished giving him the names and asking him to repeat them, she finished her tea and closed her eyes.

Morgan decided she was done for the day when she didn't immediately open her eyes again. He quietly finished his tea and started towards the deerskin door. "Abini!" The voice commanded from behind him. Startled, he turned and said, "Abini, tomorrow". Then he made sure the door opening was covered so no wind could enter the hogan. He returned to the trailer where his aunt Mosi lived and told her about sitting with the old woman and drinking tea and getting the language lesson. She smiled and told him he was lucky. Grandmother didn't talk to too many people anymore. She didn't even know how old Grandmother was. She had lived in the hogan and sat before her fire since Mosi herself had been little. Her grandmother had been called Doba. Grandmother Rozene was the maternal aunt of Doba. Mosi told Morgan that her mother had been called Popina. Mosi had never known she even had an aunt until one winter when her mother had been ill, Grandmother Rozene showed up at their hogan to care for her sister and for her children after Popina passed away. Mosi had loved the wonderful stories she would tell during the winter months.

* * *

Pain shot through Morgan's left leg as he stepped on a rock that slipped under the pressure of his weight and his ankle buckled. He had been daydreaming and had not been paying attention to the treacherous path he had been climbing down. There were so many familiar smells around him, they had dragged him into his daydreams; the scents were so strong. He partially slid down the last few feet to the canyon bottom. There, he sat on a boulder and raised his foot, feeling the immediate swelling above his boot. He knew he couldn't take his boot off. He didn't know if it was broken, but at the very least it was a bad sprain.

He felt his pockets, looking for his cell phone. Finding it, he held it up, moving it from side to side. No service. He wasn't surprised. He pulled out his radio and tried several frequencies, but he heard nothing except static. He leaned back on rock, resting from the pain. As he lay there, his talisman slipped from his shirt and hit the stone beside his ear.

Chapter 6

"Frank, you have to see this!" Mariana excitedly called to her editor. "You will not believe what I have!"

It was late at night, and most of the staff was gone for the day. Frank was still there, wrapping up the last reviews before the paper went to print. He looked up when Mariana came into his office with a set of photos in her hands. "Where's the article on the explosive ground breaking?" Frank asked, frowning when he realized that Mariana was not responding to his question.

"No, seriously, Frank, what I have here is much more 'explosive' than that ground breaking!" Mariana put the photos down in front of Frank, pushing his reviews out of the way. "Look at these!"

Frank picked up the photos, staring at the semi-blurred photos. They were in sequence, showing the start of the explosion, with the Earth flying out farther with each photo. "Okay, it's an explosion...what's so special about that?"

"NO! No ... look here, in the trees behind the explosion!" Mariana pointed to an area that was in shadow. "Look here as the explosion progresses." Frank pulled the large magnifying glass out of his drawer and looked in the shadowed area as the explosion progressed. He came to the one where the exploding Earth almost filled the photo. The light had changed, and where there had been shadow, a pale face had appeared. He looked closer. There was something wrong with the face. It was distorted in some way. He looked up at Mariana, questioningly.

"Yep, I just got proof — solid proof — of Sasquatch!" Mariana danced around the room, holding the picture with the face looking directly at him. Frank watched in amusement as Mariana finally plopped down in the chair across the desk.

"I admit, there does seem to be a face in that last picture, but what does that have to do with Sasquatch?" Frank asked her. "Besides, this is not the Pacific Northwest. Isn't that where all the Sasquatch sightings have been?"

With a mischievous grin, Mariana pulled out another set of photos, and put them on Frank's desk. "Oh, yeah? Well take a look at these. I went over to the area where I had seen the face, and this is what I found."

Frank looked at the first photo, seeing a large imprint of a foot shape on the ground, but something was out of place. He looked through the rest of the photos, realizing that it was the size and the shape that were out of place. Mariana had put her own foot next to the imprint, and the imprint was more than twice the size of hers. Frank looked up, disbelief in his eyes. "You've got to be kidding me!" Mariana shook her head and then pulled a plastic Ziploc bag out with clumps of multicolored hair inside of it.

Mariana explained, "After I took the pictures of the foot imprint, I followed the tracks. They were spread up to 4 yards apart or even farther. The creature was completely panicked at first. I found these clumps of hair in the bushes near the area. But the farther I went, the more the creature became careful of its travel. I lost the trail when it started running on boulders and rocks and didn't brush up against the bushes. The question is; what do we do now?"

Frank was assimilating the information Mariana had given him with the proof he held in his hands and comparing that with his knowledge of the rational world. Sasquatch was a myth, like aliens landing in Roswell, the Abominable Snowman and the Loch Ness Monster. His whole world was being turned upside down. He did know that most people who made claims of having seen any of them were viewed as crackpots or worse. He looked up at Mariana. "We wait," he replied. He held up his hand, and Mariana jumped angrily to her feet. He repeated, "We wait. We go back and make plaster casts of the imprints, we measure the depth and the stride, and then we send the hairs in for testing to see what/who they came from. In other words, we calm down and DO OUR RESEARCH." He said the last loudly as Mariana didn't seem to be listening. "You know that you never let out a story until you have done your research and have gathered absolute proof. What we have now is some photos, which people could say were altered. Heck, the kids in junior high could come up with something better than this." As he talked, Mariana retreated to her seat.

"OK ... sorry. I was overcome with the excitement," Mariana apologized. She was thinking now of the steps she would need to take and the research that would have to be done, all without raising suspicion from those around them. "Who do we send the hairs to, and who do we have to take the plaster casts and measurements?"

Frank organized the prints on his desk and looked closer at the hairs in the bag. It looked like there were hairs from two different creatures. Each type was of approximately the same length, but one clump was brown and coarse looking while other clumps were of varied colors and appeared to be much smoother. He looked up at Mariana, "You go do the research. What is the history behind Sasquatch? Where is he usually seen? What are the Native American myths, etc.? You know what to look for. Investigate this like you would any potential story. Tomorrow, I want you to take Amy out to the site. She knows how to make plaster casts, and I am sure that between the two of you, you can get the dimensions we need. Try to measure how high up in the bushes you found these hairs as well. I will send these hairs to a lab and see what they can tell us. I'll just make it part of an anthropological study that we are doing research on in coordination with the Museum of Northern Arizona. Above all, tell no one!"

Chapter 7

It was bitterly cold. Rozene pulled the wool blanket closer around her shoulders. She, her younger sister and her mother were huddled together under the stone overhang. They had been on the run from the white soldiers for the last three years. Their mother, Pakuna, was Apache, from the south. She had been captured in a Navajo raid when she was a young girl. Akando, the Navajo warrior who had captured her, kept her as his wife. Over time, she grew to love him and the deep canyons where they lived and traveled. Akando meant "Ambush" in the Dine language, and Pakuna always teased him that "ambushing" her was the only way that he could get her to marry him. Pakuna had given him two daughters, Rozene, meaning "Rose," and Papina, meaning "Ivy."

They had been raised in Dinetah, "the land of the People." At first, it had been good land. They hadn't been attacked when the Spaniards had marched through it. The Elders of the tribe had told stories of when the men covered in bright metal and riding large horses had conquered many lands to the south and to the east, at the pueblos.

They had helped their parents, gathering roots, berries and wood for fires. Their favorite pastime was herding the goats and playing with the dogs. Rozene and Papina were named from flowers and plants that Pakuna had seen before she had been taken from her land. Although Pakuna had learned to love her husband and the different way of life among the Dine, she also found that there were similarities between the tribes, as many of the traditions and stories were a mix learned from earlier tribes who had been diffused throughout the region during the years of drought. The Anasazi, or "Ancient Ones," had once inhabited the land, building great stone houses. But they had disappeared, leaving no trace of where they had gone.

For years, the Navajo had fought against the neighboring tribes and against the white-skinned people. Utes and Comanches would raid the Dine's villages, taking their sheep, horses and children. The soldiers had told the tribe that they must leave their lands and travel to a dry land in the east called Bosque Redondo and to Fort Sumner. Akando and several neighboring clans had refused the government orders and had fled into the badlands near the sacred mountains. It was during this time of struggle that Rozene had reached womanhood. They had been unable to celebrate with either a Kinaalda of the Dine or the NA-IH-ES, the Sunrise Ceremony of her mother's Apache people. They did what they could to honor her transition, as it was such an important step in the lives of both the Dine and the N'dee.

They arranged for one of the Dine warriors, who was not of their clan, to marry Rozene. At first she was very nervous, but her mother helped her through the rituals of both tribes, preparing her for her role as a wife and as a woman. She prepared herself as best she could. Pallaton was very strong and was a handsome warrior of the people. Her father gave her the talisman of the corn woman that he had always worn around his neck. He told her to always wear it and that it would protect her. It was a connection to the past, to one of the winter stories that she had been told by the Elders when she was younger. He reminded her that it was the hairy ones who had saved their ancestor, Laughing Boy, and that she could expect their help in times of extreme need. Their family had kept the secret, passing it to the oldest child along with the talisman.

Rozene and Pallaton were married in the springtime, as they gathered what seeds and nuts that they could, searching through the ruins of the fields that the Utes, the Comanches or the soldiers had torched the year before. There were fresh shoots, which they left, hoping that they would mature and be ready to harvest later in the year. Pallaton was a good husband to Rozene. He helped her with the baskets and loads as they traveled from site to site, always moving. It soon became apparent that they were to have a child.

Even through the trials and hardships that they were facing, the new life growing within Rozene gave them all hope.

They were now deep into the badlands at a semi-permanent camp. They had found some sheep grazing that summer and brought them with them as they foraged and hid from the soldiers. It had just started snowing, and Rozene was coping with trying to keep the blanket around her growing body. She could feel the baby within her kick weakly. She had not been able to eat regularly, especially in the last few weeks.

Suddenly, shouts were heard and shots echoed through the canyon. The white soldiers had tracked them to their winter quarters. The Dine warriors came into view, running from the soldiers. Another shot rang out and Rozene screamed as Pallaton fell to the ground, red blossoming on his back. Additional shots rang out until all of the men placed their weapons on the ground and the women had come out of the overhang. Rozene ran to Pallaton, turning him to see if he was alive. One of the soldiers ran up and pushed Rozene away, fearing that she was running to get the downed Indian's weapon. He didn't realize the she was simply running to her husband — or that she was pregnant.

Rozene cried out, feeling a sharp pain as she was pushed onto her stomach on the rocks, her talisman swinging out and knocking against the stones. Immediately, she felt a gush of warm fluid down her legs and fainted, knowing that she had lost both husband and child. The soldiers rounded up the other women and children that were in their group, forcing them the gather up their meager belongings and form into a line. In rudimentary Navajo, they were told by the Ute guide who had helped track their group that they would be walking to the Bosque Redondo camp. The men were stripped of their knives and other weapons. The women gathered what blankets and food that they could. Pakuna found Akando with Papina. The swirling snow was obscuring everything within a few feet in front of them. She yelled Rozene's name until the soldiers realized that there was someone unaccounted for. Near the body of Pallaton, they found Rozene, alive but weak, her blanket and the snow around her stained red from her miscarriage. Pakuna sobbed as the soldiers pulled her away, ignoring Rozene, knowing that if she wasn't already dead that she soon would be.

* * *

Their sleeping cave rang with the sound of stone hitting stone. Ailiya could feel the reverberations through the ground, awakening her from her winter's sleep. It wasn't time for them to awaken ... something had happened. Thaena was already up, gathering what first aid supplies she could find and picking up several buffalo skins and hides. Grandpa was awake, but Thaena told him that it was too far for him to travel, but that he could gather wood and bark from the surrounding snow-covered woods for treatment. Their sleeping cave was an old lava tube; the far end of it was much warmer than the exterior.

Thaena handed Ailiya several blankets to carry and foot coverings to protect them from the snow and sharp rocks. Thaena explained that something had happened to someone descended from Laughing Boy. The talisman Thaena was wearing was the other half of the one that Laughing Boy had given to his oldest child when he left to find his own mate. It had been many years since any of the people had sought their help. Thaena helped Ailiya put on snowshoes and removed the rocks from the front of cave before putting on hers. Ailiya was a little sleepy, kind of in a stupor, following Thaena out of the lava tube.

Ailiya looked up into the sky as snowflakes fell. There had been a fresh snow, and several inches were covering the tops of nearby boulders. Ailiya had never been out of the sleeping cave so early in the year. She was thrilled by the white landscape that spread out in front of her. Thaena could feel the talisman pulling her in a straight line to wherever she was needed. If they had to sidetrack or if they found an easier way, she would be guided back so that they were heading generally toward the northeast, toward the badlands.

It took them six hours of walking in a steady pace, removing the snowshoes when the snow wasn't deep, to reach the bloody site. Thaena stepped past several snow-covered bodies until she reached Rozene. She was still alive, but barely. It appeared as though she had been knocked out when she fell and hit her head on the stones. Thaena realized that Rozene had been with child. She asked Ailiya to start a fire and to start the healing stew. Thaena cleaned Rozene and with a prayer, wrapped the small body of the baby boy that Rozene had lost. She placed him next to the body that Rozene had been lying against.

The snow had stopped and a pale winter sun shone on them. Ailiya had helped wrap Rozene in one of the soft deerskins and then wrapped a heavy buffalo hide around her. Ailiya saw the talisman that Laughing Boy had carved and given to his oldest son around the neck of the small girl — woman, Ailiya corrected herself — as she had been with child. Although she was very pale, the young woman's eyes were fluttering and she was moaning in pain. Rozene opened her eyes. Everything was blurry, and she hurt everywhere. There was an emptiness within her. When she reached to feel for her baby, she met only buffalo robes. Tears dripped down her cheeks as she closed her eyes. Thaena moved beside her, putting her hands to each side of Rozene's face. Closing her eyes, she felt for the source of Rozene's self, to shore it up, to help fan the flames to bring her back. Seeing the carnage and feeling the pain that Rozene had experienced, she understood that the warrior to her left had been Rozene's husband and that the rest of her family was gone, on "The Long Walk" to Bosque Redondo.

The white men had been herding the Dine from their land for the past four years and containing them at Bosque Redondo. Akando had kept his family out of their clutches for four years, but the white men had finally caught up to their loose-knit group of family and clan members. It was the winter of 1867, Akando's family was among the last to be collected and taken to the concentration camp.

From her connection with Rozene, Thaena was able to calm and soothe the young woman, who had only seen 12 winters. She was also able to prepare her for the sight of herself and Ailiya. As she removed her hands, Rozene looked up into the beautiful blue eyes of a creature that she thought existed only in stories, to help the long winters pass. She wasn't afraid; she knew that these "people" were there to help her, not to harm her. More tears leaked out of her eyes as she saw the body of her husband lying beyond the fire with the small bundle she knew was their child.

Ailiya finished the warming stew and sat next to Rozene. She began feeding her small spoonfuls of the healing broth that she had made. Rozene looked at Ailiya and between spoons, she managed to say, "A-E-YA?" Ailiya grinned, feeding Rozene another spoonful. She said, "A-E-LE-YA". Rozene then pronounced her own name and asked her a question in Navajo. When Ailiya frowned, Rozene tried the same question in Apache. Still, Ailiya didn't understand. She then reached out and touched Rozene on the side of her head that hadn't been bruised when she fell on the rocks. Rozene closed her eyes and asked again in Navajo, but this time Ailiya was able to see the questions that Rozene had running through her head, primarily, "Why have you come?" Ailiya reached down and held up Rozene's talisman and then pointed to the one around her mother's neck. Rozene's eyes widened as she realized they had known she was in trouble and they came to save her, just as her father had told her when he had given her the talisman before she was married. She smiled in understanding at Ailiya and refused anymore of the healing soup. Ailiya had brewed a stew that had ingredients that reduced Rozene's pain and had made her sleepy.

While Ailiya was feeding Rozene, Thaena was

gathering materials to build a crude shelter to protect Rozene from the elements until she was strong enough to be moved. She also started to dig a large hole to inter the murdered warriors. She dug a separate hole for Pallaton and the unnamed baby.

When Rozene next awoke, she saw the warriors lined up ready to be buried, with Pallaton and their baby placed on his chest. Thaena put her palm again to Rozene's head, telling her that she needed to bury the bodies. Rozene nodded her head and said, "Akando. The name of my baby should be Akando, after my father." Ailiya helped Rozene sit up as Thaena went to the bodies and recited their traditional burial prayer and gave offerings of sacred cornmeal to each of the four cardinal directions, and for each of those who had been killed. Rozene leaned weakly against Ailiya while Thaena completed the burials of Pallaton and baby Akando first. Ailiya laid her back down on the pallet as she sobbed for the loss of her husband and child and for all of those who were now lost to her. By the time Thaena completed her duty, Rozene was asleep again.

It was two days before Thaena felt that it was safe to move Rozene. They had been periodically feeding her from the nourishing stew and melting snow for water. Thaena changed the amounts and types of herbs, depending on the need she felt when she examined Rozene. The color was coming back to her cheeks, and the swollen knot and bruise on her forehead was fading. Thaena formed a stretcher that was supported on the shoulders of both her and Ailiya, so that they could transport Rozene back to the sleeping cave. When Rozene awoke the next morning, they fed her a final meal and then gathered up what belongings they could find to take with them. They placed Rozene onto the stretcher and then lifted the stretcher to sit comfortably, with Thaena leading the way back to the sleeping cave. They rested periodically, more for Rozene's sake than for theirs. Thaena had reserved the remaining soup and put it into a deerskin bag, lined with a deer's bladder to make it waterproof. At each stop, they would encourage Rozene to drink as much as she could. She did, but although Thaena and Ailiya were careful not to jostle Rozene more than necessary, the swaying motion, in addition to her recent head injury and miscarriage, had made her feel continuously nauseous. Thaena and Ailiya spent the time by naming the plants, animals and features around them in their own language. Rozene would point at something and Ailiya would give her the name in her language, and Rozene would give the name in Navajo and Apache. Many times there were words that were very similar to each other. Thaena believed that all languages eventually went back to their own language, as they had been in the land first and the smooth-skinned people developed their language using theirs as a base. Through the millennia, there had been significant changes, but Ailiya was able to brush her hand to Rozene's head when they had confusions about the plants.

The closer they got to the sacred mountains, the more agitated Rozene became. Ailiya calmed her and told her that they lived at the base of the sacred mountains. Rozene explained that only the medicine men traveled to the sacred mountains to gather the herbs important to their tribe. Ailiya reassured her that the spirits their tribe prayed to understood her needs and the mountain would be a safe place for her to heal and to live.

* * *

It took them a full day to travel back to the sleeping cave. Halfway back, Thaena added some sleeping mixture to Rozene's drink to ease Rozene's travel discomfort. It saddened Ailiya as she didn't have Rozene to help her pass the time. Instead, she talked to her mother, about what the white soldiers had done and what had happened to the tribes. She had been confused when, each spring, they had awakened to find fewer of 'The People' in the many empty pueblos and stone houses. There were also fewer of their kind. It had been almost 100 seasons since she had seen another Elo-ai-ne, meaning "of the Earth." That is what they called themselves. Other tribes called them by various names, with most tribes and the white men calling them Sasquatch. Thaena went over the history of their people as they traveled. As a long-lived people, they often lived for more than 5,000 winters. Age-wise, Ailiya was just younger than the young woman she was carrying. The Elo-ai-ne didn't mate as early as "The People" as they didn't mature as fast. It often took the Elo-ai-ne about 1,500 winters before they were mature enough to seek out a mate. Ailiya was still learning about her family's history. A lot of the things that she knew were born into her. She had been born with an innate sense of the natural world, of the plants and herbs that grew and of the healing nature of each. She was able to communicate with any creature by simply touching it and "seeing" the communication. Most of her kind were characterized by a strong desire to wander. There were several families that did not have this characterization. Those were the ones that were sent to the various key places of travel as they had been, to provide a safe location for rest.

Thaena asked Ailiya if she remembered her visit to the large depression in the Earth that had been caused by a rock from the sky. Ailiya remembered the trip. She had several clear stones that she had collected. By touching the center of the sunken depression, she was able to "see" the pain the Earth felt when the stone had impacted it. She could feel the explosion, the force of the winds and the utter devastation for much distance around the impact. She had picked up the clear stones. The "remembrance" of the stones was of incredible heat and pressure caused by the impact. She did not know what they had been transformed into. Her grandfather told her that other stones, formed deep in the Earth, were known as diamonds. Thaena told her that their family had lived near the mountains when the stone had hit the Earth. Because they were on the mountains, they could look out and see the large cloud of debris that was thrown up into the sky. They felt the shockwave almost immediately and could feel the great pain of the Earth. It took several weeks for the heat to cool, the dust to clear and the smoke from the fires to die out before their ancestors had been able to approach the deep crater. The closer they had gotten to the impact zone, the more damage they had found. The burned, decomposing bodies of bison, mammoths, sloths, camels and smaller mammals were found. The plains were blackened for as far as they could see.

They were used to upheavals on the Earth, as they had actually been sent to that portion of the world to help warn others of their kind about travel restrictions. Most of the Elo-ai-ne traveled as solitary males or as small families. Even during the time when the Earth's crust was still moving and there were large, lizard-type animals that ranged the single continent, the Elo-ai-ne had been travelers. When the "skin" of the Earth had finished the great movements, groups of their kind were spread throughout the surface of the planet. It had been another impact that had killed out the large reptiles and most of the mammals. Because the Elo-ai-ne can feel the Earth, they could tell when and where nearby volcanic activity or Earthquakes would shake the ground. Most of the larger families were able to avoid the areas of the Earth that would be the most dangerous to them.

By the time they had discussed the history of their family in the area, Rozene was beginning to stir. Thaena and Ailiya had to make one final stop to put their snowshoes back on in order to traverse the deepening snow. Rozene was alert by the time they reached the lava tube opening. They could feel the heat emanating from the tube and knew that Grandfather had felt them coming. He had started a fire, and the smells of a hearty stew made Ailiya's stomach rumble. They had hurried after Rozene had fallen asleep in order to make it to the lava tube by nightfall. Although their vision was very good in low light, it would have been difficult to travel through the forest and snow, burdened as they were with Rozene's stretcher.

Grandfather met them at opening, helping Thaena first and then Ailiya remove their snowshoes, without putting down the stretcher again. Rozene gazed at Grandfather; his pelt had turned almost completely white. He moved slowly now, as he had seen almost 5,500 winters. Thaena did not know of anyone who was older than Grandfather. He smiled down at Rozene and patted her head. "You are with us now, little one; we are your family," he said in their language. Rozene was able to understand him, because of the pats on her head. She also understood the great age of Grandfather. When she asked what his name was, he answered, "Child, I am so old that I don't even remember what my name was! Just call me Grandfather."

* * *

Rozene healed and spent the rest of the winter months resting and learning the language of the Elo-ai-ne. She was mainly cared for and visited with Grandfather. Thaena and Ailiya needed more sleep, and Thaena awoke only periodically to check on Rozene.

Grandfather taught her the history of his people. He told her about the great animals that used to roam the grasslands. He told her of seeing Sunset Crater literally explode into being and in having to evade the slower moving lava that had made its way out of the base. He also told her of the trips he had made to the Pueblo peoples, especially the one to Chaco Canyon, to meet with their Elders. He and Thaena knew that a hard time would be coming; the Earth was going to be drier, and it would be more difficult for the neighboring tribes because their food would not grow. Rozene looked up at him curiously and said, "There are large footprints on the wall in a room at Pueblo Bonito. They show six toes."

Grandfather laughed, holding up his own foot, showing five toes. The old shaman, at the time of his visit, was a good friend of Grandfather's. He had traveled to the Sacred Mountains many times, but this was the first time Grandfather had traveled to the ceremonial center of the Pueblo people. The leaders met with him and heard him tell of the hard times that would be coming. Grandfather told the leaders that it would last for more than one generation, at least. While the leaders conferred and decided where they should have their people go, the old shaman had asked Grandfather to have his feet outlined on the wall as a memory of the day that an Elo-ai-ne had sought out the people. It was a joke between the old shaman and Grandfather. The old shaman had the recorder add an extra toe to the footprint, because Grandfather was so big, the shaman thought he should have had another toe to help him stay upright!

Grandfather had traveled to other concentrations of "The People". He advised the Elders on which directions other clans and tribes were going. Almost all of "The People" would be heading east, toward the prairie lands. He explained that he had been the one to travel as Ryone, his son. Thaena and Ailiya were needed at the great convocation. At first they resisted him. But, as this was the first contact that one of the Elo-ai-ne had initiated, they eventually heeded his wisdom, and by the time he had traveled to the land known as Mexico, most had left the area around the Sacred Mountains. He had traveled far, reaching areas to the east, north and south. Many of the communities were pueblo-style; others were cliff dwellings. All had heard of the revered Elo-ai-ne and their ability to understand different languages the land and the plants. The various peoples started making preparations to abandon their current homes and travel distances so that they might have available food supplies and the necessary, life-giving water.

Rozene passed the time sewing bags and vests for Thaena and Ailiya. She also sewed padded moccasins for Grandfather. His feet were hurting him. He had lived to such a great age that his body was slowly shutting down. The energy he received from Rozene helped make his last winters more comfortable.

It was several years later when Rozene was out gathering herbs and flowers when she heard gunshots and saw strange lights in the sky. She followed the sounds cautiously, looking up as Thaena and Ailiya caught up to her. They neared the area to the south of the Sacred Mountains where a spring burbled out of the side of the hill. They saw a group of white men in strange clothes. Rozene noted that they weren't wearing the clothing of the soldiers, but of mountain men. They had stripped the branches from a tall pine tree and hung a flag from it. The next night, after the men had moved on, Rozene, Thaena and Ailiya walked up to the stripped pine tree with the flag still flying. The bark had been removed near the base of the tree. Carved into the cleared area were the numbers "1876." Ailiya traced the numbers with her fingers, wondering what the significance was. Thaena looked at Ailiya and said, "They were celebrating the independence of the white men from the country across the big sea. I have been listening to the groups of white men who have been coming through here. We are going to have to be more careful about leaving the caves."

Each winter season, Rozene lived in a small hogan that Thaena and Ailiya helped her make near their winter cave. It was snug and kept her warm. She spent her winter months making baskets and clay bowls. More white men and women came to the southern area of the Sacred Mountains. They started calling the mountains "The San Francisco Peaks." Rozene would trade her baskets and leather goods for additional foods and beads. She eventually heard that her family had returned to their land in Canyon de Chelly. They had been released from the concentration camp at Bosque Redondo not long after they had been captured. The government had reached an agreement with the Navajos and had set aside a portion of their land as a reservation and released those from Bosque Redondo to return to that land in 1868. They were also given supplies, horses and sheep to help them start their lives again. It had taken many years for Rozene to meet another member of her clan. It took the coming of the train through the settlement that was now called Flagstaff. By the white man's years, it was 1900 when Rozene was told that her sister Papina was ill. With tears, she decided that she needed to return to her family to care for Papina and her children.

When she approached Grandfather, he told her that he would not make it through the winter season, that he had truly enjoyed knowing her and that he appreciated all of the padded moccasins that she had made for him. She had known his time would be coming soon; through the years he just seemed to fade away. Even during the summer season, he didn't often leave the sleeping cave, instead remaining on his bed of soft skins and buffalo hides.

They traveled at night, Rozene walking this time at her pace. It took them several days to find the canyon where her family had settled. Before entering the hogan, Thaena reminded her about her talisman; if she ever needed help, they would be there.

Chapter 8

The sound of stone striking stone rang through her cave, startling Ailiya. She reached into the bowl that held her talisman. It was warm to the touch, indicating that someone who had the other half needed help. Concentrating, Ailiya felt this was a new person. It wasn't Doba, the last of Laughing Boy's family that she had known. She felt physical pain in her ankle, so she determined that whoever held the other talisman would require physical assistance.

Out of several boxes and sealed bowls, she gathered healing moss and other ingredients that she mixed in a small pouch and then added water. She also gathered several rolls of leather to be used to stabilize a broken leg, if that was the case. She glanced around the cave, not feeling that she needed anything else, and walked out onto the stone ledge to get a sense of where she needed to go. Surprised, she realized that the injured person was not far away and was in the canyon. She cleared the trail to the bottom so that it would be easy to bring the injured person up to her cave.

Opening up all of her senses, she felt for the world around her. She knew where the animals were. She sent out a call for Ona, asking him to go ahead of her. She generally tried not to open her senses so wide anymore. There were too many people — there was too much movement of the Earth, too much pain. She was able to dampen the general pain and distraction that was now what she considered to be normal and focused in on the pain of the man, as well as his location. Ona shrieked from overhead, swooping down to land on her shoulder. He reported that there was a man on the rocks up ahead.

She gradually withdrew her senses, knowing that if she shut down immediately it had the effect of leaving her disoriented. It had been a hard lesson to learn, but then, all of her lessons were hard anymore. Without her mother, she was on her own even in this crowded place of the world. It had been almost 50 years since she'd had regular contact with other sentient beings. Ona chirped angrily and pecked Ailiya's ear. She reached up and soothed Ona's feathers, apologizing for not considering him a sentient being. She described to him that by sentient being she meant one of the people or her mother. Ona hadn't been hatched when Thaena had left this world, so he didn't understand about Ailiya's longing for another of her kind.

She sent Ona on ahead to land near the injured man. The pain he felt was becoming stronger to her. She did not feel his pain as actual pain to herself, but rather she could feel the pain emanating from the direction of the injured man.

She did not know which one of Morgan's descendents she would soon be meeting, but she was glad that the talisman had once again been passed down so that she could help. The last time she had been called to help was when Rozene was ready to return to the Earth.

Her mother had already passed from the Earth and had been cremated as was their tradition. Ailiya had spread her mother's ashes at several of their planting locations. By doing this, she would literally provide nourishment through her passing to the plants and that would in turn provide nourishment to her daughter.

She had felt her own talisman grow warm one winter; it had awakened her with its warmth. It was still early winter — there was no snow on the ground. She knew Rozene needed her. Because there were more people, Ailiya had to be careful in going to the hogan where Rozene had lived for the past 65 years. There were several new structures in front of the small canyon where Rozene's hogan was protected from the strong western winds.

She called to Rozene in her language and then carefully entered the hogan as the deerskin was slightly pulled away from the sides. Ailiya looked at the small, withered woman who had once run through flowered fields with her. Rozene's eyes were still sharp and they brightened as she saw Ailiya. Beside her, half asleep, was a small boy.

Rozene took off her talisman and placed it around the young boy's neck. She spoke to him softly in Navajo, thanking him for sharing tea with an old woman and for listening to her stories. She told him that the "hairy one" — Ailiya grimaced at that one — would always be available for him if he needed her. She told him that she was leaving to go visit with their ancestors and she didn't want them to ruin her hogan. Navajo tradition dictated that if someone died within their hogan that a hole was knocked through the north wall to remove the body and then abandoned. She told the boy that he could have her hogan and the many special gifts within.

Rozene knew Ailiya would be there that night, so she had asked Morgan to stay late. She had added extra herbs to his tea so that he was drowsy, but not really asleep or awake. She wanted him to know how much he had meant to her and the importance of the trust that she was placing in his hands. He nodded at her and at Ailiya. Rozene had told him many stories about the "hairy ones," so he was not surprised to see the embodiment of one of the stories in real life. He held the talisman with both hands, feeling the warmth as it spread throughout him, and he fell asleep.

Ailiya carefully picked up Rozene and managed to back out of the hogan without damaging anything. Once outside, she arranged Rozene in a carrier and returned to the sleeping cave. They talked about the changes in the world that they had seen. Rozene told Ailiya that it was 1965. Rozene believed that she was about 110 years old, but that she was just a young child compared to Ailiya who was almost 2,000 years old! Once back at the cave, Rozene asked Ailiya for one of her favorite candies that was made from prickly pear fruit. After enjoying the candy, she lay down and thanked Ailiya for saving her so many years ago. She closed her eyes and Ailiya felt her spirit slip away from her body. Ailiya said a blessing and placed Rozene's body on the pyre she had prepared before she had left to bring Rozene home.

As the flames licked at the fabric of Rozene's traditional clothing of velvet skirt with satin top and beaded shawl, Ailiya closed her eyes, missing the ones who had meant so much to her. She added herbs to the fire, blessings to the one above. Her senses were open. She could feel distant reverberations from others of her kind, but less intensely than when she had laid the pyre for her mother a few short seasons before. There was one that was closer than the others, but it felt familiar in some way. She sighed. Tomorrow she would gather the ashes and mix them with the soil of the same planting areas where they had placed Grandfather's, and where she had placed her mother's ashes.

* * *

Morgan felt the strange warmth coming from his talisman again. It was different this time, not painful, although he had been surprised at the loud noise from the talisman hitting the stone when it fell out of his shirt. He placed it back under his shirt and wondered how he was going to get out of this one. As steep as the canyon had looked coming down, it was nothing compared to how steep it seemed to be looking back up toward the top.

He knew enough first aid to know that he was in trouble. If his ankle wasn't broken, it was certainly one of the worst sprains he had ever experienced. He looked around, trying to find some wood that would make sufficient splints, as well as something long enough to work as a crutch. He knew he needed to hurry as it was starting to get dark. Soon there would be no way for him to maneuver up the canyon to the slope which decreased sufficiently in order for him to reach the mesa above.

As he sat up, he was startled by the screech of a hawk, which landed on a branch near him. It looked at him curiously and chirruped at him. Morgan answered the bird, cocking his head to the side and saying, "Well, how are you going to help me?" The hawk screeched again and took off from the branch, heading back down the canyon.

Morgan watched the hawk fly off, wondering at the encounter. Shaking his head, the recalled the stories his Grandmother Rozene had told him about Navajo history and the part that animals and birds played in the creation story. There was a nagging memory, at the back of his mind. He remembered the last night he had spent with Grandmother Rozene. He had always been confused as to what had happened that night. He remembered her giving him the talisman and saying that the "hairy one" would always be there for him. He had told his Aunt Mosi the next morning that Grandmother Rozene had been carried away by a hairy giant. He showed her the talisman and told her that Grandmother Rozene had given him the hogan. Together, they had walked to the hogan and saw the deep impressions of large feet, approaching and leaving. Mosi had heard the stories and knew that her aunt Doba had left when Mosi was little to "take care of the hairy ones." She took Morgan back to the trailer, and they called his parents. They arrived a week later, and Morgan took them back to the hogan. They had been surprised at the quantity and quality of the various baskets, jewelry and rugs. There seemed to be a great deal of different stored herbs and drying herbs. It took several days of talking with Mosi and other close relatives to determine who Grandmother Rozene had been.

They were surprised when Morgan told them some of the stories that Grandmother Rozene had told him. They looked at the years that the stories had occurred and realized that she had been about 110 years old! Morgan's parents checked the Indian records that showed the dates that her family had been brought to the concentration camp at Bosque Redondo and the family members' names and ages. Rozene had only been about 12 when she had married Pallaton. Her sister Papina, Morgan's great-grandmother, had been much younger than Rozene. They found pictures of the family without Rozene at the concentration camp and wondered where she had been. Mosi remembered that her aunt Doba had told her that Rozene had returned to the reservation to care for Papina around 1900.

His parents took him back out in the field with them, and the stories started to fade away. He continued to wear the talisman throughout his life, sometimes more out of habit than out of tradition. He hadn't returned to his Aunt Mosi's house or the hogan since that time. There never seemed to be time. He knew that Mosi still lived on the land and that periodically she had asked him about the hogan and what he wanted to have done. When he made it out of this canyon, he would make a special trip to the hogan and see what remained.

The light was fading, even faster it seemed,

when he saw a large shadow coming toward him from the canyon. He rubbed his eyes, thinking the pain was making him hallucinate. As the creature drew closer, his mind immediately remembered the scene when Grandmother Rozene had left her hogan in the arms of the large hairy creature she had said would watch over him if he ever needed help.

Light fell on the face of the creature. It was at least seven feet tall and covered in long hair. He knew this creature! He had seen those blue eyes gaze upon him when he was but a small boy. The hawk that had screeched at him was sitting calmly on the shoulders of the "hairy one" that his Grandmother Rozene had talked about and had introduced him to. The talisman about his neck warmed considerably, sending waves of contentment through him as though to let him know that everything was okay and that the "hairy one" was there to help him.

The creature put a ball of herbs into his hand and motioned for him to put it in his cheek. As his vision faded from pain and from what must have been some sort of sedative in the herbs, he felt the creature lift him up, heard the clang as his talisman joined to a similar one hanging from the creature's neck and then was blissfully unaware of the next half-hour as he was transported away.

* * *

Finally! Web jumped to his feet as he felt the small tingle from the piece of lodestone that he had embedded in a chunk of turquoise and silver. He had waited so many years that he feared he would not live long enough to see the end of his quest. Walter Edwin Barnsworth III, had searched for the creature since he was five years old. He had spent most of his life honing his skills in anticipation of this day. He was no longer as strong as he had been in his prime, but he was more fit and active than most men in their '40s.

"Umberto!" he called, "It's time! Gather the supplies and cancel all appointments for the next month. This time she won't get away!"

* * *

The darkness had stirred. Something had happened. There had been many turns around the sun since IT had awakened. IT searched around, trying to determine what had brought IT to consciousness this time.

As IT moved through the cavern, IT felt through the rocks, feeling for the touch of the hated creatures, the ones that weren't animals, but weren't men. IT had fed on these creatures since IT had been created.

Very faintly, IT sensed at least two of the creatures in contact with each other. IT shivered in excitement. There had been no contact since the great energy had pulsed through the Earth and IT had been able to consume many of the hated creatures.

Slowly, ever so slowly, IT began to flow across the bones of small and large creatures who had had the bad luck to enter the cave and have their spirit absorbed by the darkness, feeding IT, keeping IT alive.

* * *

"So, how was your date with Scott?" Amy asked Mariana.

Mariana rolled her eyes, "Ugh ... I think it is time that you stop setting me up with your artist friends. We just don't function on the same plane!"

Amy had picked Mariana up that morning, prompted by Frank, who told her the whole story when he got home last night. Out of the three, Amy was actually the one most open to the idea of Sasquatch. She was much easier to convince than Frank. She was excited to take Mariana back to the blast site and to collect some plaster casts of the large foot impressions. She often used plaster and plaster casts in her abstract art. She would use the casts either in sculptures or as part of a dimensional painting. By using pine cones, leaves, twigs, branches and other local native plants, she incorporated a part of the land into everything she created.

Since Amy and Frank never had children, the couple adopted Mariana as one of their own. Unfortunately, from Mariana's standpoint, that meant trying to set her up with many of the local bachelors. Mariana was in no hurry to settle down. She was still learning to live by herself in the slower pace of Flagstaff. She found that she enjoyed being out in the woods and visiting the various Native American ruins in and around Flagstaff. It was a different way of life than the hectic lifestyle she had grown up with and lived in Los Angeles.

Mariana had been up most of the night, working from her home laptop, researching Sasquatch sightings and information. On the way out to the construction site, Mariana filled Amy in on the information that she had collected. "Did you know that there are consistent reports of a Sasquatch-type creature on all continents of the world? I had always thought that they were only found in the Pacific Northwest. So had Frank. There are all kinds of reports, some saying they are a vicious creature, others that they are benevolent. There were also many accounts of a Sasquatch creature in most of the various Native American tribes. They thought of them as an 'Elder Brother', feeling that their presence was a warning of perilous times and that they were often of assistance when someone was sick or hurt. There were even stories from mountain men who said that when they were trapped during the winter, families of these creatures took them supplies and food that kept them alive until they were able to make their way out of the mountain in the spring."

"Wow. That is a lot of information for one night's research. Did you even go to sleep last night?" Amy glanced over at Mariana, who had printed out most of her research and had it organized in a binder. She was flipping back and forth, looking at all the information, trying to determine where the creature she had seen fit into the world of myths, legends and hoaxes.

"Yeah, actually I did get some sleep." The bags beneath her eyes belied her words, but she was so keyed up and excited that her eyes sparkled with energy. Mariana flipped to a page that showed a photo of three six-toed petroglyphs at Chaco Canyon, on a back wall of Pueblo Bonito, holding it so that Amy could see the picture.

"Whoa! That is so cool!" Amy had a great love of all kinds of art, including "rock art," the petroglyphs that had been left behind by many native tribes. There were kinds that were "pecked" into the desert varnish that formed on the sandstone cliffs common throughout the

Southwest. Others were incised lines, while still others had been applied with paint and stains. They were often so fluid and organic. She was already getting ideas for incorporating some of them in her art.

"Wait, it gets better!" Mariana exclaimed. She flipped to several other pages that showed various locations that had large footprints mixed with small prints among other symbols in what came to be known as Newspaper Rock. "It was believed that these locations were some sort of communication centers to the land's earlier inhabitants."

They arrived at the construction site and followed a forest service road to the other side of the previous day's excavation. Amy parked her Jeep where Mariana indicated and got out several bags for them to take with them. In addition to the supplies for measuring, there was plaster in ready-mix bags, extra water to drink and to mix in with the plaster bags, and her typical pack for going out into the woods. Like the Boy Scouts, she firmly believed in being prepared. She had a small first-aid kit, whistle, an emergency blanket and water-purification tablets.

She and Amy walked to the site where Mariana had seen the creature. Amy was very impressed with the quality of the foot imprints and set about finding the best ones. She sketched them out first and carefully measured length, width and depth.

She then mixed water into the plaster-mix bags and carefully emptied the plaster into the imprints and over the sides. With Mariana's help, they measured several of the strides, amazed at the distance between the imprints. As they followed the paths, Mariana took more photos, using the measuring tapes to provide actual scale. They found more clumps of hair, and they marveled at the difference in feel between the coarse brown fur and the fine, almost silky feel of the longer, multicolored ones.

Since it was earlier in the day, Amy had more success in following the trail to where it disappeared at the top of the cliff at Frye Canyon. Looking out across the canyon, she saw where some branches had been stripped from one of the pine trees. She pointed this out to Mariana who took more pictures.

They sat down to rest on the rocks at the top of the cliff. Amy pulled out water bottles and granola bars. She had been picking up various items as they traveled, unable to resist, with thoughts of how to incorporate them into a new series of paintings. It was sometimes hard for her to keep focused on the task at hand. She would see visions of swirls and dabs, creating paintings and sculptures in her mind before she actually started them. Mariana was very much the same, but her method was to paint with words, creating stories and reports by describing incidents and actions so those who read her works could "see" her own works.

They talked about myriad things, particularly speculating about what the creature was and what they needed to do next. Through her research, Mariana had read many conflicting reports about who or what the Sasquatch was, and she was starting to put together her own ideas, partly from her research and partly from her reporter's instinct. She had looked into those eyes; she knew that the creature was good and that she didn't mean harm. At this thought, she paused, why was she so sure the creature was a "she"? The creature could just as well be a male, a female or an it. But no, there was something in those eyes. The creature definitely was a female.

The day had gone faster than either Mariana or Amy had expected and the sun was starting to cast long shadows. They decided they had found and collected as much evidence as they could. Mariana flipped through the images on her digital camera, sure that they had traced the creature to the cliff's edge and that she must have escaped farther into the canyon. She would stop by the Forest Service office and get a topographical map for the Frye Canyon area along with the various Forest Service roads.

Chapter 9

As Ailiya checked to make sure the herbs had taken away the man's pain, she looked at his legs, ankles, feet and back to determine where the pain was coming from. A gentle wave pulsed against her as her hand passed over his left leg and ankle. The ankle was only sprained, but his tibia was broken. Laying her hands on the break, she was able to tell that it was a clean break. Setting aside her materials, she continued to hold his leg while chanting a healing prayer that her mother had taught her.

Morgan didn't even flinch as his leg bone was set. He was sitting in Grandmother Rozene's hogan, learning Navajo and the uses for the native plants. He remembered how sad he had felt when he realized that she was really gone. He and his parents would return to the Rez every few years, and they would work with his aunts to catalogue and distribute the many herbs, seeds and mixtures Grandmother Rozene left for the Elders in the tribe. His mind continued to drift as temporary splints were installed on his left leg and it was firmly wrapped in strips of soft leather.

He faded away again when Ailiya picked him up to carry him to her cave. As she did, their talismans joined together. Not with a clang this time, but with a haunting tune that seemed to reverberate throughout the very ground. This surprised Ailiya as the talisman had never responded this way. Generally, it was a clang or a ringing sound that she felt as much as she heard it. She felt some disquiet, like there were tendrils weaving themselves around her and the man, but also threads that seemed to lead south to some unknown entities. She could feel two distinct paths; both seemed familiar. But they seemed at odds with each other. There was another one, separate from the others. It felt darker and much, much older. She shook her head, concentrating on getting the man back to her cave before the herbs she had given him wore off.

* * *

It was like an invisible thread, pulling him toward his destiny. Web was thrilled, he hadn't had this much excitement since the African safari when he was almost mauled to death by a lion. His whole life had been in preparation for this one hunt. His walls were covered with hunting trophies from throughout the world. He reviewed the various hunts that had resulted in the mounted heads on his walls. His home was filled with treasures and mementos from throughout the world.

He had only been five when the incident had happened. He remembered it like it was yesterday.

The shame and embarrassment he felt that day had only been increased when he had returned to the ranch house where he was staying with his dad. He had run the whole way back home, tears streaming down his eyes from the terror he had felt. He had lost control and wet himself without even knowing it until he rushed into the library to tell his father what had happened. His father had looked at him in disgust, saying that no son of his would act as he was or would lose control of himself. He had found himself shipped off to a military school the very next day.

In response to this treatment by his father, he learned to never let any emotion show. He flourished at school, winning award after award, but never again living in the same home as his father. He became a decorated war hero, a sniper who had many notches on his knife hilt. His father had died when he had been overseas. By then, it didn't matter to him. His father had been dead to him for years. However, it did mean that the large ranch in Sedona, Arizona, became his, along with the great wealth his father had accumulated. He returned to Sedona, looking at the red rocks that surrounded the area. Their ranch was back in some canyons that required a Jeep trail to reach it.

* * *

Ona chirped encouragement to Ailiya, and she just laughed. "I know, not much farther." The man was large, but it was still not much of an exertion for Ailiya. She climbed the path to her cave, careful to not bump the man's leg against the side of the cliff or on any protruding rocks.

She laid him down on the old, wood-framed bed, with leather strips interwoven to provide a soft mattress. Doba had Ailiya help her make it when she had come to stay with her, before Thaena died. There was a soft, down-filled mattress with several buffalo skins and woven blankets. As she stood up, their talismans separated and the soft, humming sound ceased. Again, Ailiya was baffled by this reaction of their talismans. She studied the man's; his was worn, but whole. She picked up her own. The bottom portion had broken off when her mother died. She frowned. She hadn't really noticed it as she had placed it in her special basket after she and Doba had prepared her mother for her cremation and return to the Earth. At that moment, the man's eyes opened. He was able to focus a little better, which also meant that he would soon start to feel the pain of his broken leg. He looked up at Ailiya and said, "Yinishyé Morgan," (my name is Morgan) in Navajo. Ailiya looked surprised and replied softly with "Ailiya." He tried pronouncing it, but couldn't until she said, "I-e-le-ya." He nodded, remembering the night he had met her at

Grandmother Rozene's hogan, "Ahxehee', Ailiya — thank you, Ailiya".

Ona swooped in and landed on the wooden frame of the bed, chirping inquisitively to Ailiya, eyeing Morgan with curiosity. Ailiya asked him to be quiet and let her work on her patient. He chirped back, but settled down, keeping an eye over this strange creature Ailiya had brought into their cave. Ailiya was busy preparing food and drink for Morgan, as well as a poultice to put on his ankle and over the break to help with the swelling. After giving him a slightly different herb, which helped with the pain but didn't make him as sleepy, she climbed back down to the bottom of her path and recovered it to prevent accidental discovery, particularly if anyone came searching for this man.

She returned to the bed, seeing a little color coming back to Morgan's face. She smiled. At first she kind of looked scary to Morgan, but he could read the compassion in her eyes. She again placed her hands on his leg, feeling the bones already beginning to knit back together. She released the leather straps binding his leg so that she could free his ankle. As she did so, she spoke softly in the Navajo that she knew, feeling through the connection to his bones the questions that were in his mind. She answered as many as she could, but knew he wouldn't remember in the morning. She gave him a strong tea laced with herbs for shock, inflammation and for pain. As he settled back against the pillows, she removed the shoelaces of his hiking boots, waiting to remove the boot until his eyes had closed. Sprains could be even more painful than breaks and take longer to heal. Luckily the shoes that he had been wearing had prevented further damage from occurring. She applied the poultice to both the ankle and to the area of the tibia break, wrapping damp leather strips tightly around his foot and ankle up to the knee. She then placed the flat strips of wood on each side of his leg, attaching these with additional damp leather strips, knowing that as they dried, they would shrink, providing a stable cast for Morgan.

She then started a healing broth over the fire hearth, which had a natural vent through the lava and sandstone above them. She was a vegetarian and prepared a soup with seeds, corn and beans she had harvested and dried. She also mixed together some sunflower seed cakes with cornmeal that would be ready after the soup had simmered for an hour and the herbs she had given Morgan had worn off.

* * *

Mariana and Amy met Frank at Mariana's house. Frank had ordered a chicken pesto pizza from Oregano's, Mariana's favorite restaurant, and was waiting to hear of their adventures. As they ate, Mariana and Amy took turns describing their day and showing him the multiple plaster casts and bags with the various types of hair collected from the branches and bushes the creature left in its rush to get away.

Mariana felt that at first the creature had reacted with sheer terror, turning and pushing her way through the forest without regard to the signs that she was leaving behind. By the time they reached the cliff edge, they hadn't seen any tracks or found any other fur or hair caught up in the surrounding bushes. If they hadn't seen the marks at the edge of the cliff and the damaged branches on the tree in the canyon, they wouldn't have known where the creature had gone.

Mariana again went through the information she had gathered, laying out an overall picture of the history of Sasquatch, particularly their importance in Native American societies, where the creatures were looked upon as benevolent Elder Brothers. Most surprising to Frank was the fact that most of the evidence pointed to the fact that the creatures were vegetarian. "Hollywood sure has made them into bloodthirsty creatures, intent on destroying any who have seen them." Frank shook his head as he again looked at the photographs, amazed at the intelligence that he sensed in the creatures eyes.

By the time they had finished eating, the

significance of the dichotomy between the perceived image of Sasquatch and the exquisite creature that Mariana had captured digitally was wearing heavy on them. A find such as this would win Mariana a Pulitzer Prize at least, and it would bring the newspaper international recognition. But as they gazed at the eyes of the picture Mariana had taken, they were torn.

Amy spoke first. She looked up at Frank and said, "You can't print this; you can't print any of this!" Frank was surprised at the determination in her voice. She went on, "It would ruin this whole city. Hunters from all over the world would be descending on our forest, and who knows how much of the natural beauty would be ruined. I know what this find means to both of you, but we can't share it. Or, we can't share it in a traditional manner." Both Mariana and Frank were staring at her by this time. Undaunted, she continued, "What if Mariana writes a series on Sasquatch, using the information she has already gathered, identifying the creature as benevolent and kind? We continue to do our own research and attempt to find her; it is a her, I am sure of it!

At this point, Frank broke in, as she had distracted herself with identifying why she knew the creature was female. He looked at Mariana and said, "Well, it's your story. As much as I would love to break this news, Amy is right as to the amount of damage our forest and natural areas would sustain, as well as the hordes of hunters who would invade the area, possibly causing further destruction and death to anything that moves. The canyon you saw her descend into, Frye Canyon, leads into Oak Creek and eventually into Sedona. Think of that fragile ecosystem and what that many people would do to it."

Mariana had been looking thoughtful. At first, she had rejected Amy's plea, but as she listened to them both, she looked at the photographs she had taken. One look into those eyes and Amy's decision was made. "Okay, I will gather my research into a series, with one article weekly. That will give us time to see if we can find our creature. I can tie it into some sighting from up north and how it relates to the various native populations. If we never find her, then the story will just end up wrapping itself up. However, if we do find her, and if there is any way to communicate with her, then I can write my own story!"

At this, Amy and Frank looked at each other, shrugged and said that it was okay. They knew that Mariana wasn't as knowledgeable about the furor news like this would bring or about the delicate balance in their forest. As she continued her research and her physical search for the creature, they would help her gain an understanding and an appreciation for the nature around her.

* * *

She was alive! Brozan had felt the tendrils of connection through his talisman. He hadn't felt this happy in many seasons! He had done nothing but travel the continent, looking for any others of his kind.

He smiled, thinking of the last time he had seen Ailiya. It was long before the white-skinned people had entered the land. There had been a meeting of their kind, in the middle of the land that separates the north and south continents. In the way of the people, it was held in a country that was later called "Mexico," and it took place after the great drought of the north and before the men in metal, riding horses, had invaded the land.

She had been young, very young, by their years; less than 250 winters. He had felt much older. He had slept through almost 1,000 winters. It was the last great meeting of their kind. Elders and families had traveled from all over the continents to meet. There were not many youngsters; in fact, he and Ailiya had been the youngest. He knew that his parents had talked with Ailiya's parents about their pairing when Ailiya was old enough. She was too young to know what they were talking about, but he knew! He knew he didn't like the delicate-looking Ailiya. She on the other hand, was so excited to see another of her kind close to her own age that she insisted on following him everywhere.

He kept trying to hang out with the older males who were not yet paired, but she kept showing up. Finally, he was so frustrated that he had pushed her into a vat of recently gathered sap ready to be prepared into syrup! Immediately, he felt bad. His older brother had switched the vats, and instead of falling into sticky sap, she fell into a recently heated container, the hot syrup burning her skin as she cried out in pain. He shook his head. He didn't want to remember that part of his life.

She didn't follow him after that. In fact, she would run and hide from him whenever he came to apologize. He was banished from the site and traveled with Ryone, her father, to locate plants. As they were returning from their trek the next year, he found a monkey who had been injured. Ryone showed him how to care for the baby monkey and how to heal it. When they returned, she had awakened and was fitful because her pelt was still healing. Having the monkey to care for and to entertain her kept her occupied and helped Brozan obtain forgiveness. Additionally, he obtained a large piece of hematite, which he separated into three sections. He gave the two larger sections to Thaena, she took his piece, and with all three pieces held together, she performed an ancient chant, one that drew on the magnetic strength and abilities of the materials and bound them as one. Giving the smaller piece back to Brozan, she told him that the stones would always be linked. By the stones, they would know when the other needed help or when they were close by. He thanked her, knowing that the ancient chant and knowledge by which she bound the stones was not common. In fact, he had never heard of another of their kind with the skills and knowledge shown by Thaena. She held his hands as he grasped his portion and said, "Brozan, you are young and don't understand all that you have seen or heard during this meeting of our people. However, know that our kind are dwindling upon this Earth, and the time will come when my daughter will need you. See that you learn how to communicate through the energies of the Earth and that you learn to channel your immense energy into activities that will help others." With that, she released him.

He had never seen Thaena again. He had traveled the continent over, from the very south to the very north, learning from the various tribes that he met and from the Elders of his own kind. He had learned how to communicate using the energy of the Earth. He learned more. Once, he had reached a level where he was able to contact Thaena, even from thousands of miles away. He too, had been in deep connection with the Earth when the searing pain had flashed through his senses. He had felt the withdrawal of Thaena from this Earth and had never been able to contact her again. He had tried many times to contact Ailiya, but he had never found her, either physically or through the energy of the Earth. Even the strength of his talisman had been depleted, to the point that he could not find where the other two were.

Until today! Feeling his talisman pulse against his chest several times that day and then hearing the haunting tune that told him which direction to travel, let him know that Ailiya lived! He began to pack his belongings and to prepare the food that would sustain him during the long trip to reach Ailiya.

Chapter 10

Ona chirped at Ailiya, letting her know that the strange creature inside was waking up. Ailiya chuckled. She had finished preparing a meal and was in the process of preparing other foods for the next day. Some of the seeds and beans required long soaking before they would be soft and share their flavors with the freshly cut greens and flowers she had been mixing.

She turned back toward the rear of the cave, seeing Morgan struggling to sit up. She helped him to a more comfortable position before bringing out a small table and her chair and placing them by the bed. She looked at his eyes and felt the area above his ankle and the break, feeling the healing process working, prodding it here or there where it seemed blocked.

Morgan watched her through all of this, sensing her questing mind, which put answers into his head to questions he hadn't even asked yet! He finally asked her if she understood English. She sat back and said, "Yes. Your Aunt Doba taught me. I learned to read English as well. I don't read Navajo. They didn't have a written language when Doba was with me." At that, he looked surprised. He didn't remember any Aunt Doba. Ailiya answered, "She passed away before you were born. Your Grandmother Rozene sent her to me when she knew I would need help." With this, a tear dripped from her eye and she turned toward the front of the cave.

Morgan began to take stock of his surroundings. He was on a surprisingly comfortable bed, covered with a finely woven Navajo blanket. Instead of the familiar figures he had grown up with, larger spirits resembling Ailiya had been woven, telling a story that he couldn't decipher yet. Beside the bed, stone shelves had been cut from various colored sandstone, with wooden brackets embedded into the cave wall supporting the shelves. Books of many different sizes and shapes were on the shelves. Some were old, very old. There was a folio filled with drawings and paintings on what looked like vellum, probably from sheepskin or other animal skin.

As Ailiya arranged the materials she had prepared for their meal, he continued his observation of the cave. He saw the bird, Ona, sitting on a well-worn root that protruded through the side of the cave. The room was very organized, with everything stored in baskets or placed on additional shelves. The walls of the cave were covered with various furs, woven blankets and articles from all over the world. As Ailiya set the food down before them, he asked her, "Where did all of this come from?"

At that, he thought he caught an embarrassed

look on Ailiya's face. Before he could ask further, she asked if they could say a prayer. Startled, he replied, "Of course." It was a Navajo prayer, thanking the Great Father for the abundant foods, the good weather and finally for the meeting of the two of them. He didn't understand all of the words. He thought that some of them didn't sound Navajo. When he asked her, she told him that many of her prayers were a combination of English, Navajo, Apache and Elo-ai-ne. She explained that Elo-ai-ne was the name of both her own language and her own kind.

He looked down at the food and at the beautifully carved bowl and utensils, which looked out of place next to the fairly new cast-iron Dutch oven. Again, he thought he caught a look of embarrassment on Ailiya's face. She started talking to him, telling of the foods he was eating and explaining the herbs she had given to him. As they finished eating, she looked up, "I was taught that we must not intrude upon the lives of the people. The land has become so crowded with all of the people of the land, that I am unable to make my way to the traditional gathering places of materials my mother taught me to use. Many times, as I try to find my way, I find chained dogs and people staying in tents or big box vehicles. I watch them cook and I see how well these "Dutch" made their ovens, so sometimes I have taken items from these people." She looked down, afraid of how he would react.

"Ailiya," he said, "look at me. It is okay. You are all alone in a strange land, and I did not come to help you as Grandmother Rozene would have wanted me to do. For that, I am sorry. I am sorry that you have had to 'borrow' from the people." She looked up. He was smiling and looking at her copies of *The Borrower's*.

She grinned, "Yes, I kind of did get the idea from those books. But I always leave something in their place! I carve animals, bowls, plates and birds out of the wood found in the canyon." He laughed, knowing that her sense of honor was even stronger than his.

As she cleaned up, it was his turn to look embarrassed. "Um ... where are the facilities?" She looked confused so he tried, "bathroom." She pointed beside the bed at a very modern urinal for bedridden patients. He laughed, "I don't even want to know what you had to leave in exchange for this!" Laughing, she moved to the front of the cave to give him some privacy.

* * *

As Brozan traveled, his thoughts went back to the summer of 1945, by the people of the lands counting of the years. He and many others of their kind had been shocked when, on July 16, the Earth had let out a cry as though it was being torn asunder. One by one, each had joined with the energies of the Earth, seeking each other and trying to learn what had occurred.

It had been quickly found that where an island had once been, the Earth had been damaged as it had never been before. The nature of what was determined to have happened shocked many. They didn't understand how the people of the land could produce something that was so violently destructive. Through the centuries, it seemed as though the people of the land continued to search for stronger weapons and different ways to kill and torture one another.

This, however, had been something on a scale that hadn't even existed! The air, the sea, the Earth; all were affected by the forces. Brozan, Thaena and approximately 50 others of their kind from all over the Earth had linked and were deeply connected to each other and to the Earth. Brozan had suggested that Thaena withdraw, as he could sense her weakening strength. It had been hundreds of years since their first meeting. He knew that she had run out of the special herb, found only in the south continent; the one that helped with her heart. She was using various substitutes that grew in the region, but they weren't strong enough to prevent the degeneration of her heart.

At the time, he had crossed over into the frozen continent on the other side of the world. He knew that it was a time of great upheaval among the various peoples of the Earth. He had volunteered to travel to the other continent to connect with any of their kind who might still live there. Not all of their kind were able to or chose to communicate through the energies of the Earth. Many of their kind lived a solitary existence and wouldn't respond to calls from the Elders. He had been charged with seeking out those who remained. It had been a long, arduous trip, crossing many mountain ranges and frozen lands and hiding from the various people who inhabited those lands. He had not found many of their kind. He had found that the peoples of the land were starving and that many were waging war against one another. The lands he had traveled were ravaged, with many towns and cities destroyed, along with the crops and orchards that had once sustained them.

When the cry of the Earth had first reached Brozan, he was deep inside the country known by the people as Russia. He immediately headed to the mountains, to find a cave on bedrock stone. He preferred bedrock with a high iron concentration, as that helped him connect to the others through the magnetic and energy paths of the Earth. He walled himself into the cave, noting a small trickle of water that provided a drinking source for him. He arranged his things and made sure he was safe from outside interference before he entered the trance-like state necessary for communication.

While in this state, the Elo-ai-ne are at their most vulnerable. They are more aware of the grinding of tectonic plates, volcanic eruptions and the ebb and flow of the oceans as they respond to the pull of the moon. It is generally while in this state that any Elo-ai-ne have truly been seen or even captured. Once in captivity, they would sink deeply into a trance, so that their spirit left their bodies, which soon deteriorated and left no recognizable skeleton.

They were also more likely to lose themselves within the limitless depths of the Earth, the solar system, the very universe around them. Many Elo-ai-ne had delved so deep that they had never returned. Thaena warned Brozan of this danger when he finally learned the skills to sink into a trance and to connect to others of their kind through the powers of the Earth.

Through their connection, Brozan knew Thaena must be down in the red rocks of the area she said was called "Sedona." It was a remarkable land that was high in magnetic and energy forces, which were enhanced by the bowl-like shape of the overall area. Even though this boosted the strength of her connection, he could tell that the years without the necessary herbs had taken their toll. It had been many years since they had been able to travel freely about the continent, and even longer since they had been able to trade to get what she needed. It had been at the great meeting, more than 500 years before, that she had received the herbs of a rare plant found only at the headwaters of the Amazon.

* * *

"They were all there, you know — all of the movie stars." Web was talking as Umberto negotiated the Jeep through the rough trail to the ranch house in Sedona. Umberto was surprised, wondering what was wrong with Web, as he was not one to talk or to reminisce. Umberto was from Panama, a young man who had worked with the CIA to help his country. He had met Web and had since followed him around the world as a sort of assistant.

"John Wayne himself had come to town to build a set for the first movie he ever produced and starred in, *Angel and the Badman*. They built a western town, there below Coffeepot." Umberto knew that Web was referring to the sandstone formation in Sedona that resembled a coffeepot. He simply nodded and let Web talk.

"He had just been divorced and was missing his

kids. He had four of them by that time. I think he was lonely. I used to crawl all over the set they were building, always in trouble for one thing or another. Maybe I reminded him of his kids. All I know is that one day he plucked me off the ladder in the back of one of the sets. He set me down and said, "Now youngster, this set is getting to be too dangerous a place for a kid your size to be running through. I got you this here slingshot, but you only get it on two conditions. One, you stay off of the set and quit pesterin' my people, and two, you don't shoot any living animal."

"He raised his eyebrows at me then, waiting for me to answer, and I said, "Yes sir, Mr. Wayne, I promise." You see, I had wanted a slingshot for such a long time, but my dad had said that I wasn't responsible enough for one yet; that he couldn't afford all of the trouble that I would get into if I had a slingshot!" Web chuckled at this, remembering all of the things he managed to damage or break without a slingshot. Then he frowned and sighed. "I didn't live up to one of those promises. I left the set alone and would wander through the desert and cliffs around the ranch house where we was stayin. I would shoot off a rock at anything that moved. I got to be where I was pretty good at it and could nail an eagle while it was still in the air!"

Umberto glanced up at him, knowing that Web was good enough at anything he did, mainly through sheer perseverance.

"My dad was a behind-the-scenes type of guy. He would scout out locations for movies, help in the obtaining of permits or land — whatever was required. After he sent me off to military school, he became a workaholic. He bought up great plots of land, here in Sedona and elsewhere. When he was gone, the land was worth a fortune. I had them sell it all, except for this particular spot." He waved out in front of them at the picturesque view that very few people had ever seen. When he had inherited it, only a pack mule trail had existed. He brought in a small crew of workers from Panama, relatives of Umberto's, who were sent back much richer, but with the promise that they never tell of the road they carved from the stone.

His father had a small mansion built back up the canyon, well away from people; a place where he could hide from the world. Kind of like himself, thought Web. He had traveled and fought in most countries of the world, hunted in the rest. But this land and the memories it held were what captivated Web the most.

He had never brought anyone else here, not even Umberto, after the road had been built. This is where he felt the most alive, and he knew that it was where he would die. This place of refuge was now to be the center of his hunt for the creature.

* * *

As Mariana organized all of her research into a cohesive story, she wondered at the truths and myths that she had collected. During her research, she had continually run across mentions of "Newspaper Rock" in Utah, which had many different petroglyphs from various ages on the surface of the cliff. She and Amy took a day trip to the site, marveling at the variety found on the wall of the stone.

As Amy chatted with the local Navajo jewelers who had set up several shade covers with tables showing their wares, Mariana had photographed and scrutinized all of the petroglyphs. She was particularly drawn to a section on the lower right side that showed various footprints, with several small feet and with some large feet having six toes. She wondered at the discrepancy in the sizes and at the six-toed glyphs.

Together, they sat on a large stone platform, eating the lunch they brought with them. Amy recounted the stories she gathered from the natives, many telling of the history of the rock. They reviewed the petroglyphs, with their knowledge that a creature truly existed, to see if there was mention or notation on the stone face. The only anomaly that they could identify was the large, six-toed glyphs next to the small five-toed footprints chipped into the face of the sandstone.

Mariana pulled out a book she had picked up from a local bookstore in downtown Flagstaff about the history of the native peoples in the Four Corners region and turned to the section of book about Newspaper Rock. She read the information to Amy as they sat enjoying the peace of the canyon and the mystery they were trying to solve. She flipped further in the book and read about Chaco Canyon, seeing the same large, six-toed foot painted onto a wall at one of the pueblos there. She was enthralled with the history that was known, recorded and intended to inform their descendants.

They left the canyon, planning to head back to Flagstaff. When they reached a region that allowed cell-phone service, Mariana called the Forest Service department at Chaco Canyon. They informed her they were preparing to cover up the area that contained the prints she was asking about. There had been much vandalism, and in an effort to preserve the footprints, they were going to fill in the small room where they had been found. She quickly explained who she was and that she was writing a story. She asked if they could preserve the area in photographs before it was blocked from view. They agreed, if she would be able to get there that day.

Excitedly, she called up Frank to let him know

that she and Amy would be staying in New Mexico for the night and to share what they had found. He told her to take care of his wife and to make sure she took good pictures. They traveled through back roads, making a quick stop at the Four Corners monument, which is the only location in the contiguous United States where four states come together. Eating Navajo tacos on frybread, they continued their journey, reaching Chaco Canyon while the park was still open.

They were able to find the ranger to whom Mariana had spoken, Robert Sills. He talked to them and helped carry the extra camera equipment Mariana had brought; lights and tripods to get detailed photographs. He gave them an overall history of the settlement and the remarkable road system that connected the various pueblos. He noted that destruction caused by a portion of the adjacent cliff had collapsed onto the stone walls. Even when the pueblo had been in use, the area beneath that portion of the cliff had been shored up by the people of the land, who recognized the danger of the eroding sandstone above them.

Robert showed them the wall, which was found at the back of the pueblo in a small room. Amy cried aloud at the sight of the vandalism, "Who could do such a thing?" Robert told her that vandalism of the ancient petroglyphs was an ongoing problem. In an effort to protect the wall from further vandalism, the room was going to be back-filled until a time when greater protection could be afforded to the natural resources of the area.

Mariana set up her equipment as quickly as she could. They were losing daylight as the high cliffs surrounding the valley began casting long shadows upon the walls. She took overall shots and individual close-up shots of each six-toed petroglyph. She used a tape measure and asked Amy to shoot the pictures showing the overall dimensions. By then, the shadows had lengthened to the point that it would make it difficult to walk back to the car. They gathered up the photographic equipment and, with Robert in the lead, found their way back up the trail to where they had left their vehicle.

Chapter 11

Morgan awoke the next morning, slightly disoriented by both the pain and by the location. He quickly remembered where he was and what had occurred the previous day. He couldn't believe it! The stories told by Grandmother Rozene had been true. After dinner the night before, Ailiya had given him a soothing tea, which must have contained a sedative as he didn't remember much beyond that.

He looked to the side of the bed. The urinal had been emptied and cleaned. He didn't see Ona or Ailiya anywhere, so he took the opportunity to relieve himself. He then made himself comfortable in the bed, again fingering the figures woven into the blanket. He noted an older loom in the rear of the cave. It was all set up for a new weaving, with the warps in place. He noted various bundles of colored yarns in different baskets near the loom.

He was continuously surprised at the mix of old and new found within the cave. He finally noticed a plate of sunflower cakes and a tin cup with a cool fruity drink. He ate and drank as he resumed his review, seeing shelves filled with lifelike carvings of animals and baskets filled with various minerals and valuable stones. He was amazed at the quality of the baskets and other weavings on the walls.

As he finished eating, Ona swooped into the cave, landing on the foot of the bed frame. Ona cocked his head to the side and chirped at him. "Yes, Ona," said Morgan. "Let Ailiya know I am awake." At that, Ona swooped off the frame and out of the cave. Morgan could see the light reflecting into the cave, noting the front of the cave was offset from the opening, allowing the opening to be less noticeable from the outside. Ailiya had placed aged and broken pieces of mirrors and other reflective surfaces so that light penetrated into the back of the cave. He was familiar with the technique, having seen how the ancient peoples had lit their buildings on the archaeological sites he had visited with his parents. A shelf was filled with beeswax candles and several oil-filled lanterns. Modern matchboxes were placed on another shelf.

At this point, Ailiya stooped at the opening and came into the cave, smiling at Morgan. Despite her obvious great age, since she had known his Grandmother Rozene when she was but a child, her way of talking and acting reminded him of a young person, of someone of college age. There was a youthfulness about her that showed through her eyes. Her reaction last night to telling him about her "borrowing" seemed more of a child getting caught doing something she shouldn't.

She put down the basket on what was obviously her food-preparation area. It had a high shelf, with carved and polished wooden legs supporting the partly wood-surfaced top. Part of the table was a polished piece of granite, obviously used for chopping. The basket was brimming to the top with a mix of wild greens, wildflowers and wild berries. Several apples and peaches were also in the basket. He marveled at the variety. He asked her how she had gathered such a great variety of foods.

"I have several planting areas and orchards in the surrounding area," replied Ailiya. "I also have several herb gardens throughout the canyon, in areas where they receive enough sun and reflected heat from the surrounding stones to grow at higher elevations." She sorted out the foods and cut several apples into slices, saving the seeds. When Morgan asked why she saved the seeds and the pits, she replied, "The Earth gives to us all foods and grains and seeds. It is our responsibility to make use of all parts. I grow new seedlings for my orchards, or I use the seeds in my meals."

He looked thoughtful. "Grandmother Rozene had many baskets and containers filled with seeds of all kinds. We gave them to those in our tribe who kept the ancient traditions and needed various plants and seeds. Some said the plants grown from some of the seeds had not been seen on the reservation for many years."

Ailiya smiled. He was becoming more used to what was obviously a smile. "I helped your Grandmother gather seeds from all over the region, for many years. We always planted some of the seeds, and we never harvested all the plants in one area. The Earth needs the wide range in age of the plants in order to stay healthy. Your grandmother was a wonderful person. I still miss her terribly." At this she frowned and looked sad, not only remembering Grandmother Rozene, but all the others who had been in her life.

Morgan asked, "Grandmother Rozene lived to be very old by our standards ..." he paused, seeing if Ailiya would give any information. She looked at him and smiled again.

"Yes," she answered. "My mother knew of special herbs found in the southern continent which, when consumed by the people of the Earth, allowed them to live longer, healthier lives." We had a goodly supply of it, and when Rozene returned to care for your family, my mother sent most of it with her." Ailiya reached over and picked up a small, tightly woven basket. Taking the cover off, she showed him the contents and allowed him to smell the tea that Grandmother Rozene used to give him. He was amazed and happy that he was able to finally understand one of the many mysteries surrounding his family. As she prepared food, she gave him a more complete history of his family, that went back to somewhere in the early 1500s.

* * *

Ailiya realized that she was humming as she gathered food for Morgan before he woke up. She hadn't had anyone to talk with since Doba had died. Ona shrieked at her, "Yes, Ona, I know that you talk to me, but sometimes I like to talk to people." At this, Ona had swooped off. Ah, thought Ailiya, she forgot how much she enjoyed being around one of the people, especially one of Laughing Boy's descendants!

She started back to the cave when she heard Ona calling for her. She was careful to leave no trace that could be followed back to her cave. Ona told her that "the man" had awakened. It was very exciting to have someone to take care of and to talk with.

She greeted Morgan with a smile and arranged the food she had gathered on the table. It was a beautiful day outside of the cave. While the cave was lit with reflected light, she moved one of her chairs out to the entrance and, picking up Morgan, placed him carefully on the chair in the sunlight, propping up his legs to keep the damaged area elevated. She again gently placed her hands over his ankle and the broken leg bone. Both were healing quickly. She continued to give some of her energy to both locations, aiding in the healing process. Morgan had grimaced during the move out into the sun. Ailiya felt his pain, dampening it slightly before giving him some more tea, which helped to deaden the pain.

Morgan was able to soak in the sunlight, relaxing as the analgesic action of the tea took effect. Ailiya kept an eye on him as she separated all of the foods and started the soup on the fire. After refilling his tea, she pulled up a chair to sit near him at the opening. Morgan had drifted off to sleep again. While he was sleeping, Ailiya pulled out her folio of drawings and paintings. On a clean piece of vellum, she used drawing pencils obtained during one of her "borrowing" excursions. She quickly sketched the strong planes of his face, relaxed now in sleep. Ona swooped back inside the cave, awakening Morgan as he settled on his root. He looked over at Ailiya and saw her sketching. She continued, finishing her sketch and then finally showing it to Morgan.

He was surprised at the quality of her sketch, which captured his image and imbued it with a sense of strength. He asked to see the remaining sketches. She shyly handed over the folio, in which he placed the picture of himself at the beginning. He could see her skill progress, from the first simple line drawings to the current level of hauntingly beautiful portraits. He pulled out one of the first ones, carefully, as the material was very old and the drawing was barely visible. Ailiya looked at it and said, "That is Laughing Boy. He is the baby I rescued, along with Grandmother

Hummingbird. I was very young. It was he who carved both of our talismans." At this, Morgan looked down in surprise at the talisman worn around the neck of the warrior shown in the drawing.

Ailiya gave him a short history of her life in the forest area. What interested him most was the link that existed between Ailiya's family and his own. He had heard about the rescue of Grandmother Rozene and the time she had spent with Ailiya, Thaena and her Grandfather. Grandmother Rozene had sensed that great changes were coming into Ailiya and Thaena lives. She had asked her sister's daughter, Doba, to go to their cave and to learn from them.

It was soon after Doba joined them that the great explosion had torn through the energies of the Earth. Doba was still learning their language and their way of life, but she knew that Thaena had a weakened heart. Thaena had talked with her privately, letting her know that her time on this Earth was not long. She worried about Ailiya, who was so young, in their terms. Thaena had asked Doba to care for Ailiya. She told her of the book of records that she had maintained, which was stored in a stone box in the desert. Ailiya knew the location, but not the importance of the document or of the other items interred with their history.

Thaena had then told Ailiya she must travel

down into the stone area now called Sedona. She had cautioned Ailiya that this would be a deeper trance than she usually saw her in, but not to worry. Ailiya had accompanied Thaena to an area of red sandstone bedrock, in an area not traveled by many of the people.

* * *

Brozan was uneasy. Although there had been no further explosions, the effects of the blast had continued to reverberate through the Earth. He was in contact with each of the others, through all portions of the Earth. The weakest link continued to be Thaena, even though she had the most magnetically active area to assist in her connection. She had told him that she would not be long on the Earth, even if this connection gave her energy as she took it.

He knew Ailiya was keeping a watchful eye on her mother. She had not yet learned the skill of connecting to others of their kind through the energy of the Earth. While many of their kind chose to never connect to others, Ailiya's family had been part of the connection their kind had set up around the world. When she was more mature, her mother would teach her the skills of not only how to connect to the Earth and to others of their kind through this connection, but also the skills needed to keep from delving so deep that she never returned.

He did not know that at that moment, Colonel Paul Tibbets was prepping the plane he had named "Enola Gay" after his wife, for the flight that would take him into history. It was midday when the sudden pain shot through his head. It was as if he were chained to the Earth. He couldn't break the connection. In Japan, over Hiroshima, the Enola Gay had dropped the atomic bomb known as Little Boy, and the devastating effects surged through the Earth, affecting all who were connected through the magnetic fields. In Hiroshima, the bomb exploded over the city, where strong winds were created that wrought havoc as they blew out from the blast, only to be reflected back toward the city center, causing twice the damage.

Brozan was lost in a sea of pain. He could not know that he had been unconscious for many months. The Hiroshima bomb had been dropped on August 5, 1945, and another bomb, known as Fat Man, had exploded over Nagasaki on August 9, 1945. While the Elders had been connected, communicating with each other, searing pain had surged through the connection knocking all who had been connected unconscious. As he realized where he was and knew that he had been lost in the world for many days, he frantically sought a connection to the others. Brozan had been the one chosen to search the world for others of their kind. He had been the youngest and the strongest that had participated in the connection. His shrieking nerve endings and the pain he felt when he tried to connect revealed he was unable to create a new connection. He knew that if the reaction had been as strong in the others as it had been in him, then there was a good chance that many of the Elders had perished and that they, along with their great knowledge, were gone forever.

He worried most about Thaena and Ailiya. He knew that Ailiya did not have the knowledge yet to connect through the Earth's energy, but he knew that Thaena would not have survived such an onslaught. With her weakened heart and her location in one of the natural lodestone areas in the world, the connection would have killed her. Given that he was a continent away from her and that with winter upon him, his only option was to rest in the cave, gaining back his strength so he could seek out the remaining members of his kind.

* * *

It had been awhile since Web had been to the ranch. It was where all of his most important mementos had been kept. His dad had built the house, meant to blend into the countryside. The walls were of river rock and sandstone. The sturdy wood porch posts were oiled each time Web came to the ranch. The floors were all of flagstone, with fur rugs made from polar bear, grizzly bear and wild goat. Other rugs were made from wild cats: lions, tigers and jaguars. The heads of animals from all over the world were stuffed and mounted on the walls. The only photographs were those of Web with his teams and various dead or captured men and women.

He had been ruthless as a soldier. What empathy he may have had dissolved that fateful day when he was forced to resign or be dishonorably discharged. He had given his resignation and had started billing himself out as a mercenary to whoever paid the most. He didn't care which side he was on. He often fought against men he had trained. It wasn't until he learned that his father had died that he had felt the deep anger release. With the money left to him from his father, he traveled the world, this time shooting animals, not people. He found the hunting to be a soothing balm. He generally resided on an island near Panama.

The only hint of something besides his military, mercenary or hunting lives came from a large, framed poster from the movie *Angel and the Badman*. That was the film that John Wayne had been in Sedona filming when Web was a child. Web always felt a twinge of regret he had not lived up to his promise to the great man. It had been that broken promise that led to the dark path he had taken in life.

John Wayne had sent the movie poster, signed at the bottom, to Web when he found out that he had been sent to military school. Near his signature, the Duke had written, "Life is tough, but it's tougher when you're stupid." Web knew what this meant. He knew that he had disappointed not only himself and his father, but also the great actor, who had taken an interest in him when he was away from his own children. Web kept this quote close to his heart. He never broke a promise after that and had lived up to every word he made.

The poster was the first thing Web saw when he entered the foyer of the grand house. He used it as a reminder each time he returned or left the house. He walked through the house, checking for damage, while Umberto unloaded their supplies and cleaned up the house.

The sun was going down when Web sat down on the porch rocker to smoke a cigar. As the sun sank behind the red, sandstone cliffs, Web was transported back to the days of his youth. He had been a hell raiser, that was for sure. His mother had passed away with his birth, and his father had never forgiven him. He raised him, fed him and clothed him, but could not find the love Web had needed. He started sneaking away from his many nannies as soon as he could walk. By the time he was five, he would leave the house in the morning and return in time for dinner. The only time that he saw his father was when he was brought before him for some vandalism or damage he had caused in the various towns and cities where they had lived.

After the Duke had given him the slingshot, Web spent his days improving his skills; at first on inanimate objects, such as cans, rocks or windows. He quickly moved on to stalking his prey in the desert scrub and the lush greenery around Oak Creek. While his skills in using the slingshot improved, he also learned the subtle techniques of stalking and tracking while concealing his own path.

One morning, he was out early. It was hot in August. The temperature often topped 100 degrees or more in the desert. On his way home the previous night, he happened upon a small canyon off Oak Creek he had never seen before. The front of the canyon was blocked by bushes, but the small body of a young boy was able to scrabble through with only a few scratches.

He heard an odd humming noise, coming from farther up the canyon. The walls of the canyon twisted and turned, till all outside noise from the town receded. All he heard was the strange humming noise, now accompanied by an odd thrumming of the ground beneath his feet. The closer he got, the more it felt like the air was crackling around him. He slowed as he neared a large boulder, sneaking up on whatever was causing the strange noise.

As he peeked around the boulder, he saw a large creature, sitting on top of a ledge in the red cliff. He was startled. At first he didn't know what it was. But the noise and the thrumming were definitely emanating from the creature. He steadied himself against the boulder with one hand and at once felt an electrical shock go through him, causing the hair on his head to stand up. He jerked his hand away, but the humming noise and the strange electrical sparking were like fireflies all around him. Looking down, he found several rocks suitable for his slingshot.

He steadied himself as much as he could with the distractions of the sound and energy that seemed to surround him. He let loose his first rock; it hit the stone on which the creature was sitting. It had no effect on the creature whatsoever. This time he picked up a bigger rock but underestimated his pull. Instead of hitting the creature, the rock impacted the cliff above it, knocking a boulder loose. Even before the boulder hit the creature though, it arched back and screamed. When the boulder hit the creature's head, all noise stopped and the creature fell off the ledge, landing on the dry riverbed.

Startled, he ran toward the creature. He saw that the creature had landed face up and was still alive. He could see the chest move up and down and hear the labored, ragged breathing. He picked up a sturdy stick and was using it to poke the creature when he saw a strange piece of rock. He picked it up and was surprised when he felt a residual shock sizzle through him. He looked at the creature and saw a stone carving suspended on a piece of leather around the creature's neck. It had hit the stone canyon as the creature had fallen off of the ledge, and apparently a piece had been chipped off.

He grabbed the stick he had dropped when the stone chip had shocked him. He was starting to poke the creature again when the creature opened its eyes. Blue eyes, rimmed with red, spilled over with tears. At that moment, he heard a roar and saw another creature racing toward him. He was so shocked and scared that he had dropped his stick and fallen backward, tripping and falling onto his back as the smaller creature roared at him.

He scooted backward on the sands of the riverbed, trying to get away from the creatures. The second creature threw itself down next to the one he had been poking. Tears were flowing down her face as she lifted up the older creature, cradling her close to her chest, and began carrying her back up the canyon away from Web.

When he saw that the creature was not going to chase him, he turned over and ran as hard as he could back to the ranch where he and his father were staying. He burst into his dad's study, hoping that he would still be there, when he realized that the room was filled with men, listening to the radio. He heard something about a bomb and Japan and he yelled for his dad to come get the creature. His father was furious with his behavior. He hauled him by the arm back into the foyer, asking him what nonsense he was talking about this time and scolding him for interrupting him in a conference. Didn't he know that greater events were going on in the world than whatever mischief Web had managed to get into that day already?

When the door closed on the library, his dad looked him up and down and released him. "How dare you act like this, bursting into a meeting, screaming like a little girl and … " he glanced down at Web's pants, "… wetting your pants at your age." Web had never seen his father so furious with him. It scared him, and he was ashamed of losing control. He tried to explain to his father what had happened, but his father just yelled for Web's nanny to come and get him cleaned up.

The next day, he was awakened by his nanny, with the news that he was being sent back east to a military school and his bags were already packed.

He followed her out of the house and meekly got into the vehicle. He never saw or talked to his father again. But he never forgot the shame and the sheer terror that he had experienced, nor the creatures who had caused it.

Chapter 12

Morgan looked compassionately on Ailiya as she finished the story of hearing the awful scream of her mother as the force of the bomb surged through those who were connected with the Earth's energies. It had been almost twice the power when it reached Thaena because of the extreme magnetic and energy properties found in the Sedona area. Ailiya had recounted how she had found a young child poking her mother with a stick. She had roared at him as she had picked her mother up in her arms.

Her mother had still been alive, but just barely. Ailiya rushed back to the cave, placing Thaena on the bed they had just made for Doba. Doba had been alerted through Ailiya's calls. Thaena lay on the bed, trying to find her way back. She knew that a great power had exploded onto the Earth's surface. She was actually lucky that she had been knocked off of her ledge by the stone. If she had remained where she was, she didn't think she would have survived another minute. She had felt the pain of the others and the loss of their connection as the power surged throughout the Earth. Slowly, she felt her chest move up and down with her ragged breaths. She was aware of the surface they had placed her on. She turned toward Ailiya, who knelt by the bed, tears streaming down her face. Through her connection to Thaena, she knew the damage to her heart was too severe, that she would not survive. "Oh, Ailiya," she thought. "There are so many things that I have not taught you, I can't leave you alone like this." Memories, history, thoughts and love poured out of Thaena and into Ailiya. Ailiya couldn't understand or comprehend all that her mother was transferring to her, but she put it aside, knowing that she would be able to recall all of the knowledge when needed and when she was old enough to understand.

Morgan was amazed. If his history was correct, the power surges were due to the bombs dropped on Hiroshima and Nagasaki with the first one from the test bomb they blew up on Trinity Island. He was putting the timeline together in his head, amazed that Ailiya had continued to stay in the area, with no family. He handed the folio back to Ailiya, who went into the cave to put it safely away. It gave her time to get control over her emotions.

When she returned, she brought out sliced fruit, a cracker-like bread and a nut-butter spread. She again blessed the food and they ate. As they ate, he asked her about the orchards and gardens that she had planted. With this, she brightened up. She recounted the many micro gardens that she had spread out through the canyon and surrounding canyons.

He laughed when she asked him if he knew

how Sedona got its name. He had a basic idea, but wanted to hear the "real" truth. She said it started with her gardens and orchards. The native peoples had long since left the land, not returning back to the area where she lived. One day, she found one of the white-skinned men, near death. He had found one of her gardens and the adjacent orchard. Both were ripe for harvesting, which is why she had been in that part of the canyon. Before the area was settled, she and her mother had lived much closer to the mountain and this garden was in what came to be known as Oak Creek Canyon.

She nursed the man, giving him water mixed with juice at first. As he started to revive, she gathered a bunch of the beans, nuts and fruit and left them beside him. She moved back into the canyon and watched over him, making sure that he revived enough to care for himself. When he did, she harvested part of the garden and the orchards at night, taking them back to her mother.

A year later, when she returned, she found that the man had built a house and had enlarged the garden. A few years later, she found that a couple, the man's daughter and her husband, had joined her father. They eventually built a general store and ran a hotel out of their home. More and more white-skinned people were moving into the area. The man's daughter had been named Sedona. Ailiya found out later that that was also what they named the town when they applied for postal service.

Morgan laughed again. He was beginning to pick up the sense of humor that Ailiya possessed, as well as her compassionate nature toward others. He relaxed back into his chair, drifting away again into a nap.

* * *

While Morgan drifted off into sleep, after another judicious amount of sedative in his juice drink, Ailiya began to clean up from their meal and to start the soup onto a slow boil. She resumed her seat, looking at the talisman about his neck. She saw where it had originally been joined to hers. The scrutiny also caused her to look at hers more closely. After her mother had died, Ailiya had removed the talisman and placed it in the hair basket that Grandmother Hummingbird had made for her all those years ago.

She hadn't noticed it at the time, but the bottom of her talisman was chipped, and a piece was missing. It was on the back, so she hadn't paid it any attention between the tears in her eyes and the overload of knowledge that was rolling around in her head. She tried to remember when the talisman had been chipped. She didn't think it had been chipped before the accident, her mother would have told her. So, it must have been when she had fallen off of the stone ledge when that horrible child had been poking her mother. She rubbed her thumbs softly across the chipped area, feeling a shiver of cold run down her spine.

Could it be that little boy had picked up the chip of stone? She remembered the tendrils she felt, when hers and Morgan's talismans had joined. She moved and sat herself on the floor of the cave, going into a light trance, to feel the Earth around her. She started at her cave, feeling outward. She sensed the throbbing of nerves and muscles in Morgan's leg and the tendril that connected her talisman to his. She sensed several other threads, one so deep and dark that she naturally pulled away from it, not knowing why and not wanting to know why. The next thread was weak, but it seemed to be emitting a soft, golden light. She traveled down this path, feeling the warmth and ... love? She was surprised and pulled back. The link remained, but she went to the next one.

This thread was definitely a threat. It was linked to her talisman and the threat was close. She couldn't get a good read on it; there was too much magnetic and energy interference. This meant he was somewhere close by, such that the great magnetic and energy power of the Sedona area was involved. She pulled quickly away from this thread, knowing that it was something that would have to be dealt with but that didn't need her attention right then.

Finally, there was a fuzzy link that seemed to lead from both Morgan's and her talismans. She wondered if it was somehow connected to her being seen and causing Morgan to come searching for her. This link wasn't evil and it didn't appear to be dangerous, but the possibility existed that it could become such.

Through her trance, she felt the soft presence of Morgan awaken, with pain throbbing through his leg and ankle. Slowly, she pulled herself out of the links and the trance, being careful not to withdraw too quickly as that often left her dizzy and light-headed. She could still feel a sense of urgency in all of the links, except the one that she had veered away from. She opened her eyes to find Morgan watching her with curious eyes. She stood up and picked up his cup, moving into the cave to refill it and to add more analgesic to the mixture so that the pain wouldn't return as quickly. When she went back to Morgan he asked, "What were you doing?" While he sipped on juice, she placed her hands over the break in his leg and over his ankle, pushing and prodding the energy to heal faster and to remove any swelling. He could feel the difference when she was done, but he didn't know if it was from her ministering to him or if it was due to the drink.

"Both," she answered. She had felt his question

and answered him before he could ask. She went on to tell him about the energy fields in the Earth and how important the Sedona area was. There were many places in the Earth that had strong magnetic or energy emanations. But, Sedona was one of the few that contained both because of the unique makeup of the sandstone, the circular erosion that had occurred, forming an inverted bowl shape, and the high iron content of the stone.

She had already told him about her mother's special ability to delve deeply into the Earth, something not many of their kind could do or would choose to do. She had been able to link and communicate with others on the other side of the world. There had once been a great communication link between their kind on all of the continents. It was the increase of the peoples of the land who did not respect their kind that had caused communication breakdown and the decrease of their numbers. The ones who remained were solitary in nature and existed that way, allowing their species to almost die out. Ailiya had not been in contact with any of her kind since her mother had died, except... She paused in her thinking. That one, the golden thread, felt like it was a connection to one of her kind.

"When did your species begin?" Morgan asked. "I mean, do you know about the different stories of evolution and creation of the white people and the stories from the Navajo, Hopi and Apache?" Ailiya looked confused.

She thought for a moment and then said, "We have always been here. The father of us all created our Earth. He created the plants and animals throughout the Earth. We were created, and then the hairless ones were formed. We have always been the teachers and the helpers with men. Many of the native tribes held us in high esteem, as their Elder Brothers. The men that came later, the ones riding horses, wearing armor and uniforms, they did not respect us. They hunted us until we withdrew. Now, I usually only go out night so that I won't be seen."

Morgan said, "What about there being no sign of your kind, and no fossilized bones or skeletal remains? How could you have always been here? Man hasn't always been here."

Ailiya replied thoughtfully, "I do not know all of our history. My mother had secured our history in a stone box in the desert. I have never retrieved it. Our skeletons, once our spirit has left, quickly disintegrate, leaving no trace. My Grandfather told me of his grandfather seeing the great missile from the sky that made the crater to the east of the great mountains. He also said his grandfather used to run with the woolly mammoths and other creatures that no longer exist." She pointed behind him to a finely carved mammoth tusk. "He started that, as a recording of our family. One member from each generation adds a row. I haven't added my row yet. What I know is that the animals, birds, fish and insects were all formed first, then we were made and finally the hairless men were formed."

* * *

Brozan was in his prime. He had traveled the world over, searching for others of his kind. There was a group that had settled into the northwest of the American continent. Not many were left on the other continents. He knew of several in Nepal and Tibet, which the locals called "Yeti." He also knew of one or two who had traveled to the great island that was later named Australia. The people of the land called the creatures "Yowie." Another group had been in China and they were called "Yeren."

Those in China were from the oldest tribes. It had been one of them who had helped him after the explosion; one who had been alerted by one of the Elders who had not been in contact during the great explosions. It had taken years before Brozan had revived his strength and his mind. It took more years before he was strong enough to attempt the crossing to the Alaskan portion of the American continent. As he had traveled down the coast, he had stayed for several years with the group in the state called Washington. Here were the remaining Elders, who had helped to heal the last of Brozan's damaged spirit, mind and strength. He continued to connect to try to find Thaena and Ailiya, but he had no luck.

He traveled to the area known as Sedona, but could not sense, nor find any sign of Thaena or Ailiya. He had traveled on, to the southernmost portion of the American continent, finding peace in the mountains of the Andes in Chile. Several families of Elo-ai-ne lived in the region, and he learned of their history and traditions. He had also explored the forests of the Amazon, sad at the destruction he saw. He was unable to find the plant that had produced the special herb that was so efficacious for Thaena. He had then gone back to the crumbling ruin that the Elo-ai-ne had built in Mexico for their great convocation. It was here that he stayed, gathering food and herbs, and spending his time recording the knowledge gained by Thaena, as well as the knowledge learned from the various members of his kind throughout the world, in case something happened to him and the knowledge was forever lost.

When the Elders had been asked about Thaena, they were unable to give him an answer. They had not connected to the Earth since the great explosions took place, and then as even greater bombs were tested. They told him of a strange creature who had engulfed the ones connected during the explosion. They were unable to break the connection between the Earth's energies and the ones connected. One by one, the strange creature had engulfed them and then they had simply dissolved as the creature sank back through the energies of the Earth. The Elders had heard of such a creature, but it had been dormant for so long that it had been believed to have left the Earth. It was the one creature of the Earth that they could not understand or communicate with.

When Brozan had connected to Ailiya, he had felt the stirrings of this dark creature. Ailiya's power and understanding was not yet strong enough to attract it to her, but his were. As he traveled, he was careful not to tune into that energy, using a method he remembered Thaena had told him to use when the touch of this creature was felt.

* * *

IT moved at night, almost like a fog, following the paths, moving over water, constantly in search of the creatures.

When the Earth was formed, the Great Father organized all of the materials of the universe. As the volcanoes were formed and erupted, water was formed, in between the violent up thrusts of the Earth. In the water, the smallest of organisms began to be organized.

The great animals were formed first; different animals at different eons, the ones that could survive in the super-heated Earth, with low oxygen. It was a moist, hot world with many gasses still swirling, making up what would become the atmosphere. The laws of the universe allowed the developing planet to be bombarded by random material, left over from the formation. It took eons before the atmosphere had cooled to the point that the conditions necessary for the introduction of humans were right. The remaining animals were formed, which were made for the Earth after the major impacts had affected the life cycle of the large creatures known later as dinosaurs. Some species evolved to handle the change in the Earth, others didn't. The mammals of the land and of the oceans were then formed.

After the animals were formed, the Great Father created the Elo-ai-ne, who were to be a connection between the animals and the men, which he formed last. Unlike man, the Elo-ai-ne were able to communicate to the animals, to the Earth and to man.

Before man was formed on the land, there was a great war between the spirits of the Great Father, causing much distress. Many of the spirits, for whom the Earth had been prepared, left the presence of the Great Father. These would never receive a body, and their anger eventually turned to hatred and later to evil. As they left the presence of the Great Father, the leader, the one who started the war, had gathered various materials that had been left over from the formation of the Earth. Into this viscous material, he endowed knowledge, giving the entity, IT, a great hatred for the creatures that the Great Father had formed. Man was then formed on the Earth, but the entity was not able to harm them. IT spent its time creeping, seeping and moving through and over the Earth in search of the creatures that IT could kill.

As knowledge was given to IT, anger, hatred and evil was introduced to the land. Once IT received knowledge, IT's abhorrence of the men who walked the land grew. The fact that they had a body, a spirit and knowledge fueled IT's anger so that it sought the creatures, the ones who had also been given a body, a spirit and knowledge, but were not men. These creatures he could wipe from the face of the land, absorbing their energies and their knowledge.

IT had been in a state of stasis for many decades, awakening only when creatures stumbled into the substance that made up the entity. Since the great explosions, when so many of the creatures were in connection through the energies of the Earth, IT had been almost sated. The trance connection of the creatures locked them into the energies of the Earth when the explosion had left them helpless. IT had then had a feeding frenzy, sending multiple tendrils along the energy paths and absorbing almost 50 of the creatures. IT had then retreated to the cave to bask in the knowledge and energy IT had absorbed.

Chapter 13

Morgan awoke the next day, feeling much better. He and Ailiya had eaten a savory soup she had simmering for most of the previous day, along with a fruit pudding that was absolutely delicious. Morgan was amazed at the variety and tastes of the food and drink Ailiya had been providing for him, not to mention the natural medicines with which she had been treating him. He was healing much more quickly than if he had gone to a traditional hospital and had a cast placed on his leg.

Ailiya was not in the cave, but the urinal was clean and placed by the side of his bed. He heard a chirp and looked up to see Ona watching him from the end of the bed. Ona cocked his head and chirped again. Morgan replied, "Yes, I am up, you can let Ailiya know." With that, Ona turned and swooped out of the cave.

Beside the bed, Morgan saw a pair of carved crutches. Next to that was the table, with another plate of sunflower seed cakes and a cup of fruit juice. He enjoyed the cakes and made use of the urinal before testing out the crutches and carefully making his way out to his chair and leg rest that had been placed back in the front of the cave, in the sun. He propped up his leg and relaxed back in the chair, enjoying the fresh air, the sunshine and the smells of the forest.

He didn't hear Ailiya approach until she was almost at the cave. Her pelt appeared damp as though she had taken a bath. For some reason, he was surprised. From all that he had heard about Sasquatch, they were supposed to be accompanied by a foul stench. But thinking back, noticing that Ailiya had not used as much of the sedating herbs in his morning drink, he only remembered a pleasant smell when in her presence.

As she sat down and used a wide-toothed wooden comb to straighten out her hair and her pelt, he asked her about the phenomenon. Ailiya laughed, "That is just silly. Usually when man views an Elo-ai-ne, it is his own fear he smells. Sure, we need to bathe, just like you, but there is no odor besides our own body salts and sweats." She brushed a golden powder/salve through her hair and her pelt saying, "I like the smell of flowers. I gather roses and make a mixture that softens my skin and keeps my hair soft."

Morgan looked up as she laughed, "I tried soap one time, some that I found at a campsite after the campers had left. I didn't even have to borrow it!" Morgan laughed with her and asked what had happened. She replied, "You know that deep pond in Oak Creek, below the house on the cliff? It is right next to the road, but it was a moonless night so I figured it would be safe. Unfortunately, I didn't realize how the soap would react to so much hair! I had a very difficult time getting it out of my hair and it left large bubbles in the pond. I watched the next day, and the family was so surprised the next morning when they looked down at the pool!" At this both she and Morgan laughed. Morgan could just see a dripping Ailiya watching the results of her bathing experience.

"The soap didn't agree with my skin, and I had to apply a salve all over, which was even worse! It took forever for my skin and hair to respond and to be normal again." Ailiya went on. "After that, I stayed away from man's products and stuck to making my own powders and salves as my mother and Grandmother Rozene taught me."

She continued, "One of my favorite activities was to ride down Slide Rock, especially in the spring, when the waters would flow fast. I can only do it now on moonless nights...and I can't howl anymore." At this, she looked downcast. "Once the white man began to live near the canyon, I would scare them, so I don't do it anymore. So, I started running with the coyotes. I can imitate their call, and then I can howl!" She ended with a smile.

Morgan was still chuckling when Ailiya got up to put her things away. He called after her, "Can you bring your folio back with you?" Now that he wasn't so out of it, he wanted to review her drawings more closely. She brought it back out and gave it to him as she felt over his leg. The swelling was going down in the ankle and in the break. She would re-wrap it tomorrow so that the splints remained tight and stiff.

As she sat down, Morgan started at the back of the folio and together they went through the drawings, with him asking her about the people or places represented in them. He was amazed at the clarity of the drawings of so many years. Ailiya explained that her Grandfather had developed a lacquer that he had applied to the drawings Ailiya wanted to keep. It didn't harm the various vellum or paper sheets Ailiya had drawn on, and it didn't smudge the materials she used. Most looked like she used simple carbon; probably from their fires. The newer ones were obviously created using modern pencils, as the lines were much cleaner and sharper. Color began to be introduced, at first tentatively, but then with greater confidence.

Ailiya described the people and the significance they had in her life. There was an old one showing a very hunched over, silver haired Elo-ai-ne who must have been her Grandfather. The eyes were shown in detail, and they were the eyes of someone of great age, who looked at the world with humor. He looked like someone Morgan would have liked to have known.

They went through the other pictures, including

some of Grandmother Rozene and Aunt Doba as they had been while they were young. He was surprised at how beautiful his Grandmother Rozene had been. He remembered her as the wizened, tiny old woman who gave him tea and treats along with the stories of her past. Being in such proximity to Ailiya had opened those memories, and he was able to place many of the pictures with the people and locations of the stories.

He was amazed at the difference in the Peaks and the surrounding forest Ailiya had recorded. She had been born when Sunset Crater began to erupt. There were pictures of Walnut Canyon, Montezuma's Castle and the buildings at Wupatki at their peak, filled with people and energy. Not as they were today but, deteriorated with rooms destroyed and portions missing. With parents who were archaeologists, he had visited these and other sites she had drawn many times, but he had never completely comprehended the lives and the people that those buildings represented.

When finished, he handed them back to Ailiya and maneuvered himself upright with the crutches. He carefully made his way back into the cave, to the back where Ailiya had enlarged a natural crack through the rock that was used as a toilet. She had even "borrowed" some toilet paper for his use and had strung a blanket to give him privacy. A woven basket was nearby, containing herbs he had been told to sprinkle down the rock afterwards. The herbs helped cover the smell and contained some sort of dried lichen that helped break up and digest the waste.

Moving back toward the bed, he noticed artifacts that were definitively of ancient Mesoamerica origin. These definitely surprised him. He had heard Ailiya mention a trip to the south, but did not realize that it had been to Mexico. He asked her about them as he made his way back to his bed, tired since he hadn't had as much of the pain-killing herbs. He settled himself on the bed with the colorful pillows reclining against the headboard. He saw that Ona had come in and had settled himself on his tree root.

* * *

It was a chilly morning when Thaena and Ryone roused Ailiya. She was still very tired and didn't like the white wet stuff on the ground. It made her feet tingly, and she wasn't happy. She understood that something different was happening this season, but she didn't fully comprehend all of the excitement and energy that she felt from her parents.

Thaena carried Ailiya to a special travois that they had constructed that was basically a hanging basket slung between Ryone's two wolves. Straps connected it around their bodies, and Ryone had already placed inside it soft furs, some toys and some treats for Ailiya.

Ryone picked her up from Thaena's arms, suddenly tossing her into the air until she giggled and squealed. Thaena shook her head. The bond between Ryone and Ailiya was special. Finally, Ryone placed her in the travois, covering her with the furs and putting another fur over the top to block the sun from shining directly in Ailiya's eyes. After a winter of sleep, the weak sunlight still made Ailiya squint up at him.

Grandfather came over and Ailiya sat up. "Are you going on the great trip with us, Grandfather?" she asked.

Grandfather shook his head from side to side. "Not yet, Ailiya. I have some friends I need to go talk to before I get to come to the gathering." As she started to pout, with tears welling up in her eyes, Grandfather placed his finger on her nose so that she went cross-eyed. They both laughed. She had forgotten he had started doing that to her to get her attention when she was being petulant. A winter of sleep is a long time to a little Elo-ai-ne!

"No, I need to go warn some of the people of the Earth there are bad times coming. They need to make their own journeys and prepare their storage so they can survive," Grandfather explained to her. Through the cycles and the changes of the Earth, they knew drought conditions were soon to affect the land around them. In a land that had little water anyway, a drought could mean a painful death or war with other tribes over water sources.

"But why do you have to go, Grandfather?" Ailiya started to pout again, but saw Grandfather's finger pointing toward her nose. She squirmed in her cozy seat between Nozul and Lairi, the wolves her father had raised from cubs when they were abandoned. She squinted up at Grandfather. "Will you come down later?" she asked.

"Yes, as soon as I warn the people of the Earth, I will travel to meet up with you. Now, keep your eyes straight and be a good girl for your parents. It is going to be a long trip, and they will need your help." Grandfather smoothed the long hairs that had slipped forward onto her face. "I will miss you my little Aiya." Aiya meant "laughter or giggle" in Elo-ai-ne. He and Ailiya had spent a lot of time together during her short life. She always made him laugh, and he always had a twinkle in his eyes that drew others to him. "Now, be good and help when you can."

With that, Grandfather shouldered a pack and began walking east, toward the great Chaco Canyon dwellings of the people of the Earth.

Ailiya settled back down so she could watch Grandfather walk away as Nozul and Lairi began trotting after Thaena and Ryone. The gentle swaying of the travois lulled her back to sleep.

They traveled quickly, gathering roots and plants as they moved west. They were headed toward the great chasm in the Earth, where they could easily access the spring waters of the river. They were met by several other families at the crossing. Working together, they constructed several rafts made of bundled reeds and plants. Nozul and Lairi chose to travel with them, although they weren't too comfortable with the fast water.

Several times, they pulled the rafts to the shore and gathered different foods, both to take on the trip and to use as barter. As they reached the more arid, desert region, Ailiya saw strange plants that she didn't recognize. Thaena would take Ailiya to seek out various herbs and plants while the others did the more strenuous work of harvesting the yucca hearts. While the men gathered the hearts at the base of the pointy leafed desert plant, the women dug a large circular pit. They lined the pit with flat stones and built up a fire until the pit was heated. The harvested hearts were placed upon the stones, broad-leafed plants were placed on the hearts and soil was placed on top so the heat softened the succulent meat.

There were many other desert plants that Ailiya learned about, as well as the different animals, insects and snakes. She was very respectful of them and tried to communicate with them, but she hadn't learned how to speak all of the languages of the Earth.

Soon, the air took on a salty tang, and they reached a body of water that was very different than the meandering river on which they had been traveling. Ailiya was entranced by the large fish that jumped out of the water and swam beside them. Before her parents could stop her, she had jumped into the water and one of the dolphins swam up to her and was propelling her through the water. The dolphin had asked Ailiya if she wanted to swim with them, so she had jumped. After Ryone and Thaena saw that Ailiya was communicating with one of the more intelligent sea creatures, they relaxed, watching their beloved daughter swim between the creatures. Sometimes she was riding on their slick backs and sometimes being pushed backward through the water.

Thaena laughed as she told Ryone of the conversation Ailiya and Knoxu, the leader of the pod of dolphins, were having. Knoxu was telling Ailiya about his world, after he discovered she understood him. They were chattering back and forth, he telling her of the many fish in the ocean waters, describing the beautiful corals and deep-water canyons. Ailiya was telling him of her trip down the "muddy water," as Knoxu called the river. Ailiya was trying to explain what snow was to him, but it was beyond her ability to transmit. Thaena sent an image to Knoxu, and he responded by soaring high into the air above the water, while Ailiya squealed in delight.

Finally, Ryone plucked her out of the water as he saw her tiring. He could faintly hear her "talking" to the sea creatures, and their delighted squeals and clicks followed them as they continued to travel along the coast until they reached a large cove.

All of the rafts were beached, and the loads were distributed among all of the adults. There were very few younger Elo-ai-ne; none of them were near Ailiya in age. She walked mostly now, letting the wolves carry some of the supplies they brought.

They traveled many days, through very different terrain. Ailiya was entranced by the jungle greenery and the colorful birds she could see swooping through the trees. Suddenly, they reached a large stone city in the middle of the jungle. Ailiya was surprised. She had not seen buildings of this size before.

* * *

While most of their traveling companions stopped at this stone city, Ailiya, her parents and a few of the older Elo-ai-ne continued up a steep path. Upon reaching the top of a mountain, they found another stone city, smaller than the one in the valley. Here, they found even fewer young of their kind.

When they had traveled through the lower city, Ailiya had been lifted up to her father's shoulders, so that she wouldn't be crushed among the crowd of Elo-ai-ne who cheered as Thaena entered the plaza before the great temple. Pausing, Thaena waited until the crowd had hushed. She told them who she was and that she would be collecting their stories. She thanked them for traveling so far to meet with others of their kind from all over the world.

As she spoke, Thaena noted that there were very few young Elo-ai-ne among those gathered in the lower city. There were even fewer females. This worried her, as she picked up on the general feelings of the gathering. Many were disgruntled and upset that they had been asked to travel so far. Primarily, these feelings came from the young males. From the Elders of the group, she caught the fleeting warnings of older voices, cautioning against the younger ones. She made an announcement concerning fall activities, mainly of the games that would be held; competitions she hoped would help dispel some of the anger of the young males.

With that, Ryone helped her down from the pedestal and she began greeting those in the crowd. Several woven bags were produced, into which Thaena began placing the histories being handed to her. She spoke with each Elder, learning where they were from and what concerns they had. She placed her hands on their heads, cementing the knowledge contained in the various ceramics, paper and cloth histories of their people within her mind. Most had traveled from the southern continent and revealed the great numbers of the people of the land. Those from the north portion and those who crossed over from the narrow neck of land had traveled great distances. There were fewer of them, and more families were gone completely. Thaena learned of the loss of various family lines as Elo-ai-ne told the tales of sorrow and of being mistaken for animals and killed by the strange, light-colored people who were crossing the oceans.

The Elo-ai-ne had always had good relationships with the people in the various lands. They had eventually been pushed out from the land on the other side of the Earth. Many took refuge in the high, rugged mountain regions. Those that had been on the large land masses, connected in the middle where they were now meeting, had always been looked upon as the "Keepers of the Jungle/Forest." They had been revered and looked up to for guidance. The stories that were being transmitted to Thaena told of violence and of peoples of the land hunting their kind. The anger and disgruntled emotions she had felt emanating from the young males was partly due to the lack of young females of their kind. Those who were caught were mainly female, as they were either with child or had a child with them. Both would be killed, leaving the males to rage and to terrorize against those who had killed their loved ones.

What disturbed Thaena the most was the reports of those gone "rogue"; meaning they had given up their beliefs in Mother Earth and in Father Sky. They ate meat from animals and hunted the peoples of the land. They turned away from others of their kind, even causing harm to other males who entered their areas. Once they stopped the traditions, they quickly deteriorated into animal-like creatures. They forgot how to use the energy of the Earth to communicate to others of their kind and to have reverence for all living things: plants, animals, Earth and Elo-ai-ne. If this trend continued, their kind would soon disappear from the land.

When she finally reached the other end of the great plaza, Ryone put Ailiya down and got out food and drink for Thaena. He deeply loved his mate. She was so incredibly talented and yet also so incredibly frail. She did not let the others see the difficulty that she had in giving of her energy. Each person she touched and laid her hands upon went away with a piece of Thaena's energy. She tried to give them peace, to urge them to attempt changes within themselves in order to help others.

Thaena looked up graciously. "Thank you, my love." she said quietly, slipping some herb into her drink. After several minutes, Ryone was grateful to see her physically re-gather herself. Her energies were quieting, as Ailiya helped the others with them organize the histories by family, so that family groups would be put into one bag together. This activity gave Thaena and Ryone a moment of peace to discuss the problems they had observed. While Thaena could read others of their kind, as well as animals, Ryone could read the Earth. He knew of the great drought that had recently ended and of the millions of the people of the Earth who had died. He knew the great drought that had occurred in this area would soon migrate northward, affecting the great plains and mountains that he so loved.

Ryone asked her how she was as he gently caressed the top of her head, helping to relieve some of her pain and tension by drawing it away from her. He was much stronger physically, and it hurt him when he could nothing to help his mate. They looked up as Ailiya squealed. Ryone smiled fondly upon their daughter. She was like a bright light in the gloom of night. She had just deciphered what the squiggles were on the various forms of material. She had been "listening" in her mind when those she was helping with would read the family name. He shook his head; she had been told that was rude, as not all of their kind were able to do that. She was growing up so quickly, and her skills and powers would far surpass both his and Thaena's. He glanced down at Thaena, quietly resting his hands on her shoulders now, encouraging her to talk. She shook her head. "There is too much to process, my love, "she closed her eyes, "I must rest and let it settle into patterns before I can describe it to you. However, we must find something for the young males to do, now and in the future, or we will lose more of our kind." He nodded his head, accepting that while she had great weights placed upon her frail shoulders, he could provide the strength. He left her to rest in the shade and went over to see if he could help his daughter remember her manners.

* * *

As Web and Umberto settled into the ranch house, Web showed Umberto the topographical map...the size of a pool table...he had commissioned. The map was a detailed 3-D structure of the Sedona and Oak Creek area. On top of the map were red pins, which indicated supposed sightings of a Sasquatch creature. Surprisingly, there had been many in the Sedona area. Most people assume that Sasquatch was relegated to the Pacific Northwest. Web knew better. He had employed investigators throughout the world researching and documenting the many sightings of the Yeti, Sasquatch, Abominable Snowman or other unknown creatures. On the walls were plaster casts of large footprints. One wall was reserved for the "Sedona Monster," as he called her. He didn't know why he assumed it was a her, but he was confident that the creature who had terrified him as a child had been a daughter coming to the aid of her injured mother.

The map also showed most of the houses in the outlying areas of Sedona, the structures in Oak Creek Canyon and the Jeep trails through the areas. Following the road, from the top of the canyon, coming from Flagstaff, were forest service campgrounds and buildings. Overlain in color on the map was information taken from GIS sources. Particularly, Web had requested detailed vegetation information. When viewed all together, the information showed patterns that didn't match people trails, orchards or native resources. On southern cliff walls, small areas of vegetation occurred where they shouldn't be. He found small orchards, tucked up in canyons at higher elevations than would be expected. By studying the way the ancients had lived in Wupatki, he found they lived mainly on south-facing cliffs. But, micro-environments were formed because of reflected light and heat that allowed a great variety of vegetation to grow. From his close-up experience, he had seen the creature's teeth. They were flat, indicating that the creatures were omnivores. Most people believed that there wasn't enough food for a vegetarian creature, particularly in the Southwest. Exploring seeds, recipes and other traditions of nearby native communities, he found that almost every plant that grew in the canyon and in the Sedona area would be useable, either as food, medication or cording material.

He had made great studies of large apes and chimpanzees. He sponsored other studies to determine what requirements would be needed for the creatures. He found that they were intelligent, using tools to harvest foods. The majority of their diet was vegetation, consisting of fruits and vegetables. Their needs were simple: vegetation, water and shelter. What did confuse him was the lack of multiple beings in the Sedona area. Every single plaster cast was the same size and shape. He had known there were at least two creatures living in the area, but only for a while as he knew the older creature would have died soon after her fall from the cliff. Most animal species need other animals. They will go to great lengths in finding others of their kind for companionship. He was baffled why it appeared that only one remained in the area.

He explained the map to Umberto, directing him

where to place the hunting cameras they had brought with them. He had the latest models, which were tripped by movement but also transmitted live data to a base unit. Using the location of where plaster casts had been made of the great footprints, they were able to narrow their search area to several back canyons leading upward, toward the Flagstaff area. He also shared his research information with Umberto, who, until that moment, had never been given access to the full picture of the many different areas in which he had provided research or information. Web also told him the full story of his childhood encounter. With this, Umberto left to start the initial tracking and placement of the cameras. He wasn't surprised at their quarry. His country had its own traditions and stories relating to a great monster. He was surprised at the length to which Web had taken this search.

* * *

After Umberto left, Web contacted his long-time friend Dale Walters. They had both been young boys when they met at military school. Both seemed to have been abandoned by their families. It drew them together as they grew. Both served military tours of duty, but while Web had left and become a mercenary, Dale had moved up in the ranks. He had recently retired to the family land in Washington. It was Dale to whom Web had confided his story.

Growing up in Washington, Dale had heard many stories about the Sasquatch creature. He was able to help direct Web in some of his searches, giving him information that he had received through his military contacts. He and Web, out of necessity, had kept their friendship quiet. Web's mercenary activities would have had a negative effect upon Dale's military career.

Web saw the first camera connection come into the server. Umberto had set up the first one and set it to recording. Under Web's direction, Umberto had placed the cameras a minimum of six feet off of the ground so that they wouldn't be tripped by hikers or by the animals in the area. As the signals transmitted into the ranch house, Web initiated the backup connection to the computer in Dale's study. Once the connection was made, Web contacted Dale using an Internet secure site for video conferencing.

"Web! You old dog, how are you?" Dale's face filled the computer screen. "So, I take it that this is it?"

Web replied, "Yes. I received warning from the chunk knocked off the original talisman." He held up his hand, showing the ring with the lodestone embedded adjacent to the other stones. He went on, "I've got Umberto out setting up the cameras right now. You should be getting a bounced signal from each of the cameras on the link I sent you earlier. I have him setting them up in the areas we have identified as either the likely canyons where she lives, or on the paths she takes to her gardens and orchards."

"So, the GIS information was helpful?" Dale asked. "I had some quick thinking to do when I requested that information. I told them that I was thinking of retiring there and wanted to get an idea of where the best growing areas would be. Everyone knows about my greenhouses as my 'retirement' nears so they accepted the explanation."

"It was that information that helped me identify her likely food-gathering areas, although through my research I found almost everything in that canyon can be used to support her." Web sat thoughtful. "There are a lot of foods and supplies she would still need assistance in getting, just given the closed-in position in which she now finds herself. I will have to look into that to see who might be assisting her."

Dale replied, "I have heard that there is a colony of vets living in the forests near the rim over the canyon. Maybe she has connected with one of them. I will put out some feelers to see if any of those who have 'dropped off the grid' might be in that area."

"Thanks, Dale. By the way, I have put several cameras on the house, including the server closet. All are linked to our system, and if something happens all of my information and research, as well as other data, will automatically be sent to your computer. There is information in there that you haven't seen before and information from my mercenary days that may help clean up some questions ..." Web grinned. "Your Pentagon buddies may not like all of it, but it may gain you some points in the future. You won't get it unless something happens to me. If something does happen, there is information to be used in contacting my lawyers and taking care of my properties. I will need you to help Umberto if he needs it or provide money to his family if he doesn't survive."

"Web, are you planning some kind of war down there?" Dale asked incredulously. He had known of his friend's obsession, but wasn't aware of his willingness to die for it. He enjoyed hunting as much as the next guy, but not if that next guy were Web. To Web, hunting truly was like breathing. He would go down fighting rather than live incapacitated. "It's good hearing from you, but let's make sure none of these safeguards have to go down."

Web smiled again. He rubbed his thumb over

the now warm stone on the ring on his left index finger. "No, this is it old buddy. I will get her this time. I have put a net over the whole area. She won't get away."

Chapter 14

"Father!" Ailiya exclaimed excitedly, running over to him after he had stood up. "Come look at all of the wonderful drawings and words!" Her grandfather had been working with Ailiya on learning the letters of their language and on how to draw. She had a wonderful way of seeing the world around her, which extended to the way in which she recorded it.

They had not been working on her language yet, as she was still very young, but her mind was like a creek when the winter snows began to melt: She just kept searching and seeking, gathering in as much knowledge as she could, until she literally collapsed from exhaustion. In helping the others sort the family histories, she had learned much of their language and she had picked up on much of their thoughts, since neither her mother nor her father were there to block her inquisitive mind. She kept quiet on what she had learned, partly because she didn't understand all of it and partly because she had been surprised at the attention she had garnered while in the plaza.

Sitting on her father's shoulders, Ailiya was able to see over the heads of all of the other Elo-ai-ne. She was thrilled with her viewpoint and with all of the energy she could feel. Some of it was as sharp as lightning, dancing over the heads of some of the

Elders. Some was dark, and she instinctually drew back from it. She was able to understand many of the undertones because of the close contact with her father. In her eyes, she could see the energy transfer from her mother to those who clustered around her. What surprised her was the attention paid to her. After the Elders had met with Thaena and she had moved on, they had spoken to Ryone, many of them patting her legs or her hands while she sat on her father's shoulders. Small transfers of energy would happen, until it seemed like the air around her glowed. She saw how each encounter with her mother decreased the energy around her. It was also very hot in the sun of the plaza. She squirmed, uncomfortable from the heat and from all of the attention the Elders were giving her. She would catch glimpses of memories or thoughts from them, not understanding that she was the first female youth many of them had seen.

Ailiya did not know that her family was important on many different levels. The Elo-ai-ne were a people who wandered the land. Several families possessed characteristics that made them more stable than others, like her father's family. For as long as he and Grandfather could recount, their family had been in the area of the great volcanoes. Her mother's family included some of the most talented healers and teachers. Thaena was one of the last of her family. Even though they were great healers, their family line had defects of the heart. Many of them did not live long enough to mate and to have children. Thaena had lived as long as she had because of a very rare, very difficult to obtain herb that only grew in the southern continent.

Part of their family legacy was in keeping track of the families of the Elo-ai-ne and of their history, their knowledge and of the changes in the Earth around them. Ailiya gleaned much as she helped the Elders sort the family histories. Some of them were stamped onto clay tablets, which were then baked and hardened. Others were woven into fine linens. Still others were written on the materials the people of the land used in their folded books, known as codices. The materials for this paper came from the inner bark of the amate tree. The bark pages were pounded together and allowed to dry. Folded, the history was neatly kept, and a lacquer was placed over it to set the ink in the fibers. The ones Ailiya liked most were those made on thin sheets of malleable minerals. There were shiny. Some were heavier than others, but all were thin sheets. The letters of their language were incised or stamped, just like on the clay tablets. She liked rubbing her fingers softly over the top of the smooth metal sheets, feeling the light energy stored in the material by the one who wrote the history. Some were very old. She handled these with care.

She had seen her father talking with her mother as Thaena needed to rest. She ran to him only after she saw him get up. She felt slightly guilty for "peeking" into the minds of those she was helping. Her mother had sent her a soft whisper, reminding her of her manners. She grabbed her father's hand and pulled him over to various history piles, which the Elders were now putting into separate bags. "Look at these! See how differently they wrote their letters? Why is it so different? Look at these pictures! Do you think I can learn to draw like that?"

Her father swung her way up into the air, till she felt like she was flying. She was invigorated by all of the strange energy she had been around and in being in such close contact to so many others of their kind. Ryone laughed, throwing her skyward until she was laughing instead of talking. He swung her close to his chest, looking down at her flushed face, "So, little one, have you been enjoying yourself?" Mentally, he gently reminded her not to peek into the minds of others, especially because many others did not even know she had that ability.

She dropped her gaze, embarrassed. "I am sorry father," she whispered. "But there was so much information and I didn't understand it!" With that, he put her on the ground and she was off, pulling him by one hand, asking what the plants were and the animals and the insects. Finally, her excess energy expended, they walked back to where Thaena sat, quietly thinking.

As they walked up, she looked at her daughter, "So, what did you think of the stone plaza of the people?" Thaena quietly listened as a now calmer Ailiya was able to put together some of her thoughts and ask about the energy she saw. She was leaning on her mother's lap, trying to give her mother energy, but she didn't know how it flowed from Elo-ai-ne to the ground, the plants or to the animals around her. Thaena smiled, knowing of the great intellect their daughter possessed. As the bags were gathered and the group began the final trek up the mountain, Thaena held her daughter's hand and taught her how to feel the energy in herself and in everything around her. As they walked, Ailiya learned how to send little bits of energy back and forth from her mother to herself.

* * *

Ryone walked behind his mate and their daughter. He could see the small transfers of energy between the two of them. Ailiya all but glowed from all of the excitement and energy of the day's activities. She had never been around so many of their kind before. It had been more than 2,000 winters since the last great gathering; the one at which he had met his mate.

He had never traveled as far as he had for that

convocation. He was much older than Ailiya. His father had not attended that meeting. He remembered there had been much more youth of their kind. There was not the disgruntled energy that he had sensed during today's passing of the histories.

He had looked up to see the most beautiful Elo-ai-ne he had ever seen, walking among the families, accepting their histories. When it was his turn, his hand brushed hers and it was like receiving a bolt of lightning through his body. He had looked into the deepest, bluest eyes he had ever seen. As Thaena introduced herself, she placed her hand on his. This contact sent bolts through both of them. Her eyes widened at the connection. She was older than most Elo-ai-ne when they mated. She had not felt she had met the male for her. She told him later that one look into his eyes sealed her as his. She continued on, gathering the histories. One of the Elders with her asked Ryone to help them with the histories. He followed along behind her, almost in a daze. Entranced by her every movement, captivated by every word she said. He began to feel a pressure in his head. She turned around to place a history in a bag and deliberately placed her hand on his. "Open your mind," he distinctly heard, but it was with his mind, not his ears.

He shook his head as he looked at her

questioningly. "Like this." He heard the voice again distinctly and realized that it was contact directly between the two of them. He smiled at her. He had not known of this connection to others. His family was strong in connections with the energies and minerals of the Earth. "It is just a different type of energy," he heard in his mind as she moved forward again. "Just open your mind, and show me your world."

With that, they moved throughout the very large crowd. He could see she was tiring. One of the Elders with her pressed food and water into her hands while they paused. He could see the concern in those that surrounded her. Many of them were aware of the communication between he and Thaena, and they smiled at him with joy. Those who accompanied her had watched her grow to maturity, without forming the deep attachment that Elo-ai-ne made when they mated for life. They had seen and felt the sparks between Ryone and Thaena. They knew before he did the significance of that one touch.

That one touch changed his life. By the end of the convocation, he had been bound to Thaena. He learned of many of the other families and of their histories as he helped Thaena compile them into one book. He had learned of her heart condition and that she had never been expected to reach the age she had. She had an herb that had been brought to her from the southern continent, one obtained with great difficulty. The flower grew only at the headwaters of the great river. Adding to the difficulty in gathering the plant was its resemblance to the bark of the tree. It only opened in the moon of the summer solstice, when, bathed in the white light of the full moon, the blood red flower opened, bloomed for three nights only, and then closed forever. New flowers grew from the seeds of the old flower as it dried in the morning sun, leaving the seeds at the heart of the plant.

Now, looking at the exchange of energy between his beloved mate and the beautiful daughter they had created, he thanked the great father for preserving the life of Thaena and for the blessings of being a father to Ailiya, who taught him new ways of looking at life each day. Catching his thoughts, Thaena turned and smiled at him. She was just as beautiful now as she was the first time their eyes had met. Ryone smiled, sending her thoughts of love and of the wonderful massage he had planned for her. He smiled even larger as she blushed.

Ah, he couldn't believe how lucky he was. Once he had Ailiya and Thaena settled, he would start out in search of the heart plant, as the herb that had prolonged and saved Thaena's life was dwindling, and her condition was growing worse. These thoughts he was careful to block from broadcasting. His concern for his mate over shone all other concerns. Once his father arrived to help Thaena tend to Ailiya and to record the Elo-ai-ne history, he would start out on his own trek.

* * *

Brozan had seen the small female Elo-ai-ne, sitting atop her father's shoulders. He and his brother, Broene, had traveled to the convocation with the Elders in whose care they had been left when their parents had been killed. Neither one knew much about their family. They were the only young males in the entire settlement before coming to this meeting. Bypassing the main plaza, the Elders led them up the mountain, to a much smaller temple complex. Here, they were introduced to other parents with young male children. Most of the young females were already bound to males.

Given a room of their own, Brozan and Broene adapted to life in the settlement. They spent much of their time in the forests, learning of the plants, trees, animals and insect life. They also learned the hunting skills needed for protection and for the games held at the end of each season. Brozan was the youngest of the unbound males. Since they were so rarely in the plaza, they didn't see the young female for several seasons. By then, she was allowed to wander around the plaza on her own.

Unfortunately, in Brozan's eyes, she seemed to attach herself to him. Whenever he would enter the plaza, there she would be, wide blue eyes smiling at him. The other males would tease him; even his own brother would make fun of him. He began to sleep out in the forests and found himself more and more alone as he sought to avoid the little one called Ailiya. He knew that she was of some importance, but he was frustrated with being separated from the larger, older males.

Broene proposed a solution, suggested by the other males. Brozan would spend some time walking with her and then help her walk along one of the stone walls surrounding the plaza. The other males would place a vat of syrup at an opening in the wall, placing a thin board across. As she walked across the board, it would slip and she would fall into the vat. Brozan was uncomfortable with this, feeling that it was too mean, but he wanted to be included with the other males.

The other males made the arrangements and one day, Brozan walked into the plaza, up to where Ailiya was sitting. She jumped up in excitement at seeing him. She had been playing with a rag doll that he had never seen her without since her arrival. He offered to show her the other side of the temple, where there was a great history carved on the stone. He reached out his hand and she eagerly grasped it. Both yanked their hands away when visible sparks of energy erupted the moment their hands touched. Ailiya was surprised. She thought she had inadvertently sent energy to him. Brozan did not know the meaning, nor did he know you could transfer energy. He held out his hand again and she cautiously took it, making sure to keep her energy level low. A tingle still rippled between them, but it wasn't as surprising to either one. Instead, a deep feeling of contentment and warmth spread from the contact.

He walked her over to the wall that was too high for her to walk along by herself. He was quiet, concerned with the consequences of the plan. She was so excited to be talking with him that she continued to chatter away, telling him about the family histories she had been learning about. She was telling him about swimming with the dolphins and about the pictures Knoxu had put in her mind. She sent some of the images to his mind, startling him again. He almost let go of her hand. He didn't know there were those of their kind who could communicate with their minds. She was swinging her doll in the other hand, singing some of the songs the dolphins had taught her. Just as he was about to help her off of the wall, so she wouldn't fall into the sticky syrup, the stone she was walking on rolled away and she dropped over the side of the wall, falling more than 10 feet into a vat of boiling rubber.

Brozan froze, and then jumped over the side of the wall, landing on the outside of the vat. He could feel her pain! He sent out a mental yell as well as a vocal shout for help. He could hear the older males laughing from their hiding place behind the dense leaves around him as he tried to reach for Ailiya, who was screaming in pain. He managed to get a foothold up the side of the wall so that he could reach of the lip of the large stone container and pull the struggling Ailiya to safety. Her pain was intense. He had never felt something so horrible!

As he pulled her over the side, he saw that her pelt was completely saturated with the boiling rubber and that it was already beginning to harden onto her skin. Thinking quickly, he ran several feet to the closest cenote, thankful that it was full of water. Holding Ailiya's trembling, pain-filled body close to his and ignoring his own pain from the burning rubber coating his hands, he jumped into the cool water. He could feel the slight relief that it provided to Ailiya, but he also sensed that she had gone into some kind of shock. Instinctively, he reached into her mind, seeing pathways of energy that were quickly fading. He sought out the brightest spark, sending energy and thought to it, telling her to hang on, that he was sorry and that help would soon be there.

Ryone roared at the young male to hand him

Ailiya. Instead, Brozan held her closer and told Ryone, using his mind voice, to pick them both out, that Ailiya needed his connection. Ryone paused, then reached down and pulled both of them from the cenote. He picked them both up, Brozan, holding Ailiya like a baby, putting all of his energy into her to keep her with him and to dampen the pain he could feel breaking through his connection with her.

Thaena met them at the top of the plaza, having heard her daughter's screams of terror and pain. She could see the connection between Brozan and Ailiya, but Brozan didn't know how to control it. She ran beside her mate, toward their rooms, with one hand on Brozan and one on Ailiya. Simultaneously, she started blocking Brozan, directing his energy toward his own injuries, while quickly assessing what he had done for Ailiya and continuing the connection. Her daughter had slipped into a deep, shocked condition. Brozan had done what was right, even though he had had no training.

At their rooms, they left Brozan with other Elders, who tended to his own burns and to his matted pelt where he had clutched Ailiya to him. Thaena could hear his mind speak, broadcasting to everyone that he was sorry and that it wasn't supposed to have happened. She told him to relax and directed the other Elders to teach him to block his thoughts so that she could focus on Ailiya.

In Ailiya's room, they carefully laid her on the soft pad she used to play with her doll. She normally rested in a brightly colored hammock in the corner, but Thaena needed to have complete access to her small daughter. Searching Ailiya's mind, she pulled the bright spark back, while at the same time blocking the pain. She could feel Ailiya reluctantly reach out to the comfort of her mind. She remained at Ailiya's side, with both of her hands placed on either side of her head.

Ryone and several of the other healers were working on the matted pelt and burns that Ailiya had sustained. There was no way to remove the rubber. Ryone had called for the sharpest obsidian knives and for the collection of numbing ointment to treat the burns. All of Ailiya's pelt had to be carefully removed down to her skin, where blisters were already forming. Once they removed her pelt, front and back, they carefully started applying the salve to the blistered skin. At this point, Ryone moved next to his mate, taking the task of bringing Ailiya into a healthful sleep while Thaena could concentrate on blocking the pain her daughter was feeling.

* * *

Ailiya awoke to find her Grandfather looking down at her with concern. He had arrived at the temple complex right after Ailiya had been injured. He helped tend to the young male, learning from him what had happened and that it was a cruel joke made worse by the older males. He told her to go back to sleep, that she would feel better when she woke up again.

After Ailiya was fitfully sleeping, Grandfather took his turn, dampening her pain and talking to her mind, telling her of his adventures with the people of the land and of his trip down to see her. She had been carefully turned every hour so that cool, damp cloths could be placed upon the tiny, shorn body of his precious granddaughter. He had to be conscious of his thoughts, to keep any negative or angry energy from harming her further.

Several of the Elders took turns with Ailiya's family, turning her, tending to her and replacing the cloths and the ointment as needed. Only a few of the medical Elders were able to assist in dampening her pain. Thaena mixed up several cool drinks that they gave to her on a regular basis, which helped with healing and in deadening her pain.

Brozan was being treated in the other room. He was also being taught how to use his newfound talents so that he would stop broadcasting his thoughts, emotions and pain. Thaena sat with him and learned of the original trick they planned to play on Ailiya. She explained to him that she understood that he wanted to be among the older males, but she also pointed out the consequences of that desire. She sensed the raw power in him and knew that he would need someone teaching him. She didn't have his family history as it had not been written. She had to wait until she had them all together to determine where he fit within the family lines.

Once he was able care for himself, he remained in their rooms, helping to bring food, water, herbs and whatever was needed by the others for the care of Ailiya.

Chapter 15

Ryone and Brozan set out in search of the heart plant once Ailiya had drifted into an early winter sleep. The older males who had plotted and carried out the prank had been banished from the upper city. Brozan was allowed to stay so he could help care for Ailiya. He was only allowed to help when she was asleep or when she was being blocked by one of the Elders. The first time she had been awake when he brought her food and drink, she started screaming and crying hysterically.

Brozan was aware of the pain he had caused Ailiya, not only physically, but also mentally, as she was broadcasting her thoughts when she wasn't awake. He felt terrible and kept apologizing to Thaena, Ryone and Grandfather.

Thaena had several meetings with the Elders, letting them know of the great strength and capacity she felt within Brozan. It was decided that Thaena would help instruct him, as his family line had been lost. Once he gained some control, he would leave with Ryone. Thaena showed him how to "see" and to use the energy around him. She taught him basic medical care, which he was able to practice on his own injuries, as his burns had not healed completely. She was surprised when Brozan asked her about the spark of energy felt between him and Ailiya when he had first taken her hand. He hadn't felt it with anyone else. Ryone happened to pass by when Brozan asked about it. Thaena looked up into the smiling eyes of her mate, who seemed to be teasing her, waiting to see what she had to say about the traditional "signal" of compatibility. She replied that some Elo-ai-ne have a special affinity to others, the way he could see energy and could speak with his mind. She didn't go into detail that he was most likely intended as Ailiya's mate. Both were too young, and Ailiya may not have known the significance either.

At this point, Ryone took over Brozan's training. They prepared their packs for travel, including weaving bags and baskets to carry the minerals, plants and samples that they were sent to collect. Brozan was so involved with his new training and the travel preparations that he didn't recognize the growing resentment of the other males, including his own brother. Ryone did, however, and increased the pace at which they made their preparations.

Before they left, they let Brozan take a moment with Ailiya so that he could feel her pain and apologize to her, even though she had been placed into an early sleep. Thaena kept a hand on Ailiya's head and helped guide Brozan in entering Ailiya's sleep without awakening her. He blanched when he felt the great pain she still experienced. He followed Thaena's directions, sending small bits of energy to the most painful areas. Once the pain was blocked, Brozan was allowed to apologize to Ailiya's semi-consciousness. He carefully withdrew and patted Ailiya clumsily on the shoulder, on one of the few areas that hadn't been shorn.

One of the grandmothers, knowing of Ailiya's love for her doll, had formed a clay doll and fired it, sewing clothes with beads and blankets so Ailiya could have some comfort. This had been given to Brozan, and he carefully placed the wrapped doll against Ailiya, who felt the bundle and curled herself around it.

Thaena smiled. "You did well, Brozan," she said. "Remember your lessons of today and how to use them for the good of the Elo-ai-ne. You have great strength and an even greater capacity to learn as a healer." She placed a hand on his shoulder and, using mind speak, continued, "My daughter may have need of you someday. Take care to learn as much as you can."

With that, Ryone and Brozan shouldered their packs and made their way down the steep trail to the lower city. Brozan was allowed to say goodbye to his brother, Broene. Because of the uncertainty of the family line, but also because of the great strength found in Brozan, Broene was allowed back to the upper temple to assist Thaena while Ryone and Brozan were gone. Their search would keep them away from the conclave for several seasons.

As they traveled, Brozan gathered feathers from the many colorful birds that abounded in the country. He had asked one of the weavers for some of the finest fibers to be woven into a loosely woven cover. Within the loose weave, he would intertwine the feathers, as well as any colorful beads he found along the way. When Ryone asked what it was for, Brozan said, "Ailiya is very embarrassed that she doesn't have her beautiful pelt anymore. I know that it will grow back in time, but I wanted her to have something that would make her feel special and not like some kind of monster." Ryone nodded. He was glad Brozan had developed his senses so that he understood how his precious daughter felt.

They traveled through many different lands, spending shortened resting seasons, traveling the length and width of the southern continent. Finally, they reached the headwaters of the great river. Ryone had described the plant to Brozan, as well as how to gather the various plants that they encountered. Each time they harvested a plant, they offered a prayer to the Great Father. Brozan was also taught to only harvest several plants from each location, leaving the youngest and oldest plants intact. He was told it showed respect for the living energy in all things and allowed the plants to continue to grow and to flourish.

The primary difficulty in finding the heart plant

was that the bark-like exterior only opened to show the blood-red interior on the full moon at the first planting moon. The plant clung high up on the rough-barked trees and cliffs, blending in until the night the moon shone on them and allowed the plants to open up, exposing the seeds and the thick flesh of the inner petals. It was the inner petals that were needed for the medicinal uses. Ryone was also charged with trying to transplant some of the plants. In order to do this, he had to wait until right after the plants had closed again, as they basically entered a hibernation state. He and Brozan pried several of the pods off of the trees and the cliffs, placing them in long baskets, where either rock or branches had been placed. Ryone and Brozan worked carefully, encouraging the plants to reattach themselves prior to slipping into deep hibernation.

Once they had gathered the amount that could safely be harvested, without removing too many of the reproductive plants, they started back to the Elo-ai-ne gathering.

* * *

They were nearly over the mountain ranges when they heard a piteous noise coming from behind the brush. Brozan found an injured howler monkey. It had a broken leg and had been left behind by the others. Brozan examined the small monkey, feeling for its pain, as he had been taught. Sensing the break, he was able to block the pain while he set the leg. He carefully placed the monkey in one of the empty sling baskets.

Ryone watched on, verifying that Brozan was following the methods he had been taught. He was proud of the young male. He had grown much over the past seasons, both physically and mentally. He could find the various minerals that they used in their healing and ceremonies, as well as sense the areas within the Earth that emitted strong electric as well as magnetic forces.

As they traveled back, Ryone was helping Brozan learn to use those energies to communicate with Thaena. It was exciting for Brozan, as though a whole new world had opened to him! Thaena had directed them to a spot where very powerful stones would be found. Once there, Brozan chose a large stone of deep amber with black flecks. He could sense the strength within the stone. Thaena said that the stone would help in his future training.

The young howler monkey, whom Brozan named Neanthe — meaning 'little one' — recovered quickly, with Ryone and Brozan taking turns caring for him and teaching him to communicate. Neanthe liked to climb into the various bags and baskets, hiding from Ryone and Brozan, and taking great satisfaction when they pretended they couldn't find him. Ryone commented that Neanthe would be a good companion for his daughter. Brozan agreed and started to impress upon Neanthe the memories of the injured Ailiya. Neanthe, so soon after his own injury, felt sadness for the small female of the ones who had healed him. When asked if he would be a companion for the young Elo-ai-ne, Neanthe agreed the small female would have need of him.

* * *

Ailiya awakened slowly. She stretched carefully, not feeling any stretching of her recently healed skin. She smiled, tucking the blankets around the doll that she had awakened to find. Her mother, grandfather and the other Elders had helped block her pain and helped her sleep through the past several seasons.

She sent out a mental query to her mother, who calmly welcomed her daughter back to a state of activity. Ailiya carefully sat up and put her doll into the basket another of the grandmothers had woven for her after the last season. She felt through her body, the nerves were not feeling like she was on fire. Her skin itched, but the blistered, raw skin had healed. The growth of her pelt had been slow. In fact, they had to shear her pelt over the damaged areas several times in order to properly apply the healing salve. She pulled her knees up to her chin, covering herself with a blanket. She was embarrassed that she didn't have her long, beautiful hair anymore. The cool breeze also caused chills to go up and down her arms.

Thaena walked in with Grandfather and a tray of fruit and water. She smiled as she saw her daughter's alertness. It had been difficult caring for Ailiya and continuing with the collection of the history as well as the training of Broene. She sighed at the thought of Broene. He had great power, but he had no empathy for others and he felt he deserved respect from the other young males as he had been allowed back into the upper temple complex.

After eating and drinking, Ailiya asked how long she had been healing. She knew it had been a while as she was taller. When told that it had been several seasons, she was very surprised. Tired, she laid back down, pulling her doll into her arms for a short rest.

When she awoke again, she saw her father and Brozan sorting the baskets they had brought back with them. Surprised, she asked Brozan, in mind speak, what he was doing. He turned to look at her, glad that she hadn't screamed this time. She did wrap her blanket tighter around herself. Brozan looked up at Ryone for permission. Ryone nodded. Taking the carefully woven wrap, he walked slowly toward Ailiya. Using mind speak, he again apologized for her being hurt and that she had lost her pelt. Her pink skin turned even pinker. He held up the garment, telling her that she would have the most colorful pelt of anybody. The inside of the garment had been lined with the softest leathers they traded for on their way back to the settlement. She smiled shyly and thanked him. He helped her drape it over her head and showed her how it flowed down her arms and was tied at her side, to allow her to move without aggravating her skin. She touched the colorful feathers and fabric, thrilled with the colorful tunic she could wear to hide her healing skin and pelt.

As she patted the fabric, looking at the various types of feathers, beads and shells that Brozan had intertwined, she noticed a dark blur scamper up Brozan's back to jump toward the foot of her sleeping pallet. Brozan had told Neanthe that Ailiya's skin might still hurt and he was to be careful. Neanthe had hidden behind the doll basket, peering out at Brozan and then at Ailiya. Entranced, Ailiya called out to Neanthe in mind speak. She giggled and clapped her hands when the tiny monkey told her that he was going to look after her. She gently picked him up and put him on her shoulders, careful of the spots that had been tender. The tunic Brozan had made for her was thickly padded at the shoulders, to prevent rubbing or damage to her newly healed skin.

Ailiya looked up at Brozan and thanked him again. She asked him to tell her about the trip he had just made. Ryone moved to her side while Brozan settled onto the sleeping pallet, opening his bag of personal treasures he liked and that he thought Ailiya might like to see. Ryone kissed his daughter on her head, glad to see her in such good spirits. She hugged him, all the while carrying on a spirited discussion with Brozan using mind speak, seeking the pictures in his head. Ryone shook his head, knowing that he was not needed.

He set off with the remaining baskets to give to Thaena and the other healers.

* * *

Abruptly, Ailiya stopped recounting the stories of her trip as a child. She suddenly realized how tired Morgan had become and how much he was starting to hurt.

Startled, Morgan dropped back into the present time when Ailiya jumped up to get him some juice. She added more herbs for pain, since they had been talking for so long. As he drank his juice, Ailiya began preparing dinner. He had been so engrossed in her story that he didn't realize how much time had gone by.

Morgan considered all of the history he had just

learned. He had been to Teotehican, the city that Ailiya said was the lower city. He remembered touring the area with his parents and hearing stories that the complex had been built for giants by the Mayans. He didn't know where the upper temple complex was. From the description provided by Ailiya, he didn't think it had been discovered.

As Ailiya made seed cakes and battered dandelion flowers for dinner with a green salad, she continued to answer his questions. The most important one, to Morgan, was the sensation he felt when he fingered his talisman.

Ailiya explained how Brozan had brought out the beautiful stone when he was showing her the treasures. They had taken the stone to Thaena, who directed them to the stone cutter. Ailiya had been given softly padded slippers, which allowed her to carefully walk with Brozan. This time, Brozan knew the significance of the energy shock between them when he held her hand to help her up steps.

The stone cutter was one of the oldest Elders. He sat the two young Elo-ai-ne on a padded bench while he examined the stone. He twisted and turned the stone, seeing the minute fractures of the highly charged stone. Returning to his work area, he picked up a large mallet and placed a sharpened antler against the top of the fracture. With one strong blow, he split the stone into three pieces. A loud clang reverberated throughout the room. Given the nature of the stone, the three pieces remained in tight contact. He smiled at the young ones as they clapped their hands at his performance. Bowing, he handed the stones back to Brozan.

Finding Thaena, Brozan handed her the stones. As they had discussed, she bound the stones, so that there would always be a connection to the other pieces. She gave one piece to Brozan, who took it solemnly. He knew of his responsibility toward Ailiya and toward the rest of their kind. Thaena had found their family history and lineage. Broene had already permanently moved down to the lower temple to be among their family. She was still concerned about him and about the stories related to her. He was acting as though he was royalty and was demanding the other young males do his work. Returning to the stones, she told Brozan he would be able to use the stone to communicate with her. Ailiya had tired and Neanthe was pulling her toward her pallet so she could rest. Once she was lying down, Neanthe perched near her head, glaring at anyone who entered the room.

Morgan remembered the loud clang that his talisman had made when it had hit the stone and then again when Ailiya had picked him up. Ailiya set up the meal on a small table near the bed. She smiled as she saw him fingering the talisman. His was in the shape of Xilonen, the female goddess called the "Hairy One" that Laughing Boy had carved and had passed down through time. Morgan was amazed at the connections that were brought together. He knew the information he had just gained would rewrite all of the textbooks and would thoroughly shake up the scientific community, but he also knew that it couldn't be shared. If the information were to get out that Ailiya existed, she would be hunted until she was captured or killed.

* * *

Umberto returned, having placed 20 remote, solar-powered cameras and set them to transmit their pictures to the ranch house. Some of the locations had been treacherous, but he knew if he didn't place them exactly as Web had directed, he would pay for it. Through his years with Web, he had been placed in many dangerous and downright scary situations. He had always trusted Web with his life, and he had never had cause to regret that trust. His family had been made financially secure. He had been able to send his nieces and nephews to America for education. Their lives were not what his had been; terror, danger and hunger. For that he dedicated himself to Web.

For the first time, however, he was unsure of Web's choices. He had never put together all of the pieces to realize that Web's obsession was a Sasquatch! He had gazed about the canyons, forest and desert he had found himself in, placing and adjusting the cameras and the solar power arrays and verifying the wireless connections. It was such beautiful country; not like his jungle homeland, but there was something haunting about this land.

He remembered a story his grandfather had told him of the gentle creatures that Web now sought. His grandfather had been in the jungles, searching for macaws and other sought-after wildlife to sell in the markets. He had been bitten by a poisonous snake, and he was all on his own with no radio or assistance. He was almost dead, hallucinating and wishing that he were dead. His leg had swollen up until it was almost three times its normal size. He had cut the skin to allow the infection to drain out, but he knew he was dying.

He awoke to find something placing water to his lips. He drank greedily, almost crying when the container was pulled away. He knew he would be sick, but the thirst was all-consuming. He looked up in surprise to see a dark creature looking down on him. He was too weak to struggle, but gazing into the intelligent eyes, he knew the creature would not hurt him.

The creature carried him to a shelter and cared for him until he was able to return to his home.

While in the creature's care, the creature communicated with him in Spanish. He gave him medicine, food and stories of the past. Before he left, the creature gave his grandfather several stones that turned out to be worth enough to pay for the time he had lost due to his snake bite. When he returned, no one would believe his stories, except for his grandchildren. They loved hearing of the creature who had saved their grandfather.

As Umberto thought of the goodness of the creature, he knew that it was the same type of animal. Most likely it was not the same creature as his grandfather had told them the creature who had helped him was a male. He even said that his name was 'Brozan'.

Chapter 16

Mariana had been busy summarizing and correlating the vast amount of research she had gathered. She was continuously amazed at the consistency in the stories from ancient peoples that attributed a large, hairy being which was thought of as an "Elder Brother" or as a "guardian" to the people. She found stories from almost every tribe and on every continent.

She, Amy and Frank met frequently to go over different notes and to try to determine how they should proceed. Frank knew that they were sitting on a powder keg. If the news were to leak out, their story and the very life of the being was at stake.

Frank had to keep Mariana on regular stories as well, or others would start to wonder what was going on. He did have a staff of investigative reporters who paid attention to everything! He tried to give her stories that would appear to require a lot of out of office work so that she could continue her research.

Most recently was the notification that the noted Dr. Morgan Nezhoni had disappeared after a guest lecture at the engineering department at Northern Arizona University. One of his colleagues had notified the authorities when he didn't return to the university for a second lecture. The police had looked into the disappearance and discovered that his belongings were still in his hotel room, although it didn't appear as though he had been in the room since checking in the day of his lecture. Further investigation revealed that the rental vehicle had not been returned to the facility.

When two hikers discovered the rental jeep, Frank sent Mariana out to interview the hikers and to review the area where the jeep had been found. He felt it was more than a coincidence that the jeep had been found relatively near where they had lost track of the being. He ran a background check on Dr. Nezhoni, while Mariana set out to the rough dirt road where the jeep had been located. Frank discovered Dr. Nezhoni was Navajo, although he apparently didn't grow up on the reservation. His parents were both scientists, working in the archaeology fields. Dr. Nezhoni's education and experience background was impressive. He traveled throughout the world, working on many archaeology sites as well as at disaster areas, assessing and providing temporary supports for search and rescue teams.

Mariana found police along with search and rescue teams at the location of the jeep. It had been several weeks since Dr. Nezhoni's disappearance. There were no tracks left, although a game trail, leading into Frye canyon was found.

Mariana took several photographs and interviewed several of the search and rescue teams. As she prepared to leave, she saw Gene Morrow, one of the Sheriff's department's investigators. He told her it looked like Dr. Nezhoni had gone on a hike and that it didn't look like there was any foul play. She asked about Dr. Nezhoni's belongings. Thinking quickly, she told Gene that the newspaper had planned on doing a piece on Dr. Nezhoni, prior to his disappearance. She noted that Frank and Amy were friends of Morgan's. She asked if she could take his belongings to the newspaper office to be held until he was found. Gene, knowing Mariana as well as the newspaper editor and his wife said that it would be okay, after he had catalogued the items. The jeep would be returned to the rental agency and his belongings would be gathered and stored anyway.

Mariana waited until the investigators were done and then signed a receipt for Gene, acknowledging that she had accepted the belongings. Gene also directed her to the hotel where Dr. Nezhoni had been staying. His belongings had already been packed by the hotel staff and they were storing the items. On her way back to the office, she stopped by the hotel to pick up his bags. After returning to the office and speaking with Frank, she decided the white lie she had told Gene about the newspaper doing a story on the renowned engineer wasn't that much of a lie, as she was interested in the exploits of the man. The places where he had been and the work he had done was fascinating.

* * *

"Umberto! Come quick!" The excitement that Web was feeling was palpable. He had been reviewing the photos taken the night before when he spotted his prey. Proof, proof that he had been searching for his whole life was recorded on the night vision system of several of the cameras. He excitedly checked the cameras for their locations as Umberto ran into the map room.

"Hurry, help me mark which locations captured the images." Web said.

Looking up at the wall of video monitors, each one receiving images from a single camera, Umberto correlated them to the locations of each camera. After identifying each location, Umberto asked, "Sir, are you sure she is dangerous? It looks like she was gathering vegetation and fruits."

Immediately, Umberto knew he had said the wrong thing. Web slammed his fist down onto the map table, bouncing extra pins and markers so that they flew off of the map. Veins pulsing, a red faced Web glared at him. He didn't say another word, just went about picking up the pieces that had been thrown free from the table.

It took Web about an hour before he calmed

sufficiently to review the photographs again. As Umberto had said, the creature went to and from various gardens and orchards, filling woven baskets with fruit, greens and flowers. It didn't matter to him. He knew who the creature was and that she was the one responsible for the way his life had turned out. If she hadn't scared him so badly, he wouldn't have been sent to military school. He paused, revising that thought, he wouldn't have been sent to that military school at such a young age. He would have grown older under the care of his nannies, with the world as his playground. No. The creature would have to pay and she would have to pay with her life.

Chapter 17

Mariana wrote up the story on the missing engineer. Updating the story with information as results of the search were called off. Efforts to locate his immediate family were just as frustrated, as it appeared that they were in the jungles of South America. The more Mariana reviewed the information gathered on Dr. Nezhoni, the more intrigued she became. She also wondered if there was a connection between the being she had seen and the disappearance of the engineer.

She thought it was interesting that it was a Navajo who had gone missing in the location of where she knew her being had entered the canyon. Given the close proximity of the Navajo people to the area where the creature had chosen to make her home, she wondered if there had been some kind of connection between them.

Around noon every day, Mariana drove out to Frye Canyon. She generally parked near where Dr. Nezhoni's jeep had been found. She would take her lunch and whatever notes she was working on that day and enjoy the quiet peacefulness of the forest. Frequently, she noticed a hawk that seemed especially intent upon her. She started talking to it, leaving extra food for it as she ate her lunch each day. She started posing questions to the hawk, since it seemed so intelligent and focused on her.

The hawk would cock its head to the side as Mariana would talk, seeming to understand every word.

* * *

Umberto had been staked out at the rim of the canyon for two days. He had supplies, water, cameras, food and night vision lenses and goggles. Web had stationed him to this location when after a week of observation, the creature was found to travel between the two canyons almost nightly. They had even captured a few images of the creature during the day, up the canyon to his right. On the map, the canyon to his right was called 'Frye Canyon'.

Web continued scanning the footage, correlating it and making notes to himself. There had been several secure phone calls between him and Dale. When Web showed Dale the high quality video taken during the day, Dale was astounded. Even though he had grown up with the idea that Sasquatches were real, he had never truly believed it. The state of Washington even had a county where Sasquatch hunting was illegal.

Between the two of them, they reviewed the most pertinent research and information in order to determine the best plan of attack. Dale kept pushing Web to tranquilize the creature, but Web was adamant. He blamed all of the misery of his life on this one creature, on the one event that had so changed him.

At night, when Web did rest, he unconsciously rubbed the lodestone on his ring. It had continued to feel warm on his finger. Additionally, he could 'feel' the connections to the ring. Despite what he felt, there were at least two additional 'tendrils' as he thought of them. They felt distinct to him. Two of them seemed to be close to his location and to each other. The third was fainter and came from the south. However, each night, the one to the south seemed to draw closer.

* * *

Following the pathways of energy in the Earth, IT closed in upon the prey. The magnetic and energy fields of the Earth had several locations where great power resided. IT was searching in these areas for signs of the creature that he felt tapping into the energies. There was another one, one who had evaded IT's probing. This just made IT more determined to find the creatures.

The one who had awakened IT from the stasis IT had been existing in, was a female. She didn't know about the entity or at least she didn't know how to avoid letting IT know she was there. Her connections to the energies were tentative, but growing stronger each time she tapped into the power. IT was remembering a connection during the great explosions when one of the most knowledgeable of the creatures severed their connection before the tendril IT had sent towards the strong power emanations was able to reach the female. At the time, IT had so much knowledge and energy assimilated from the other creatures, IT hadn't contemplated about the one that had 'got away'.

Actually, it had been two who had 'got away'. The female had sent some sort of power surge towards a young male who had been on the other side of the world. He hadn't been able to reach the male creature either. IT felt a similarity between the creature who was constantly evading it and the male creature who had also severed its connection before IT could reach him.

Flowing along the energy pathways, IT felt a great sense of justice as the two energies appeared to be converging. With great anticipation, IT looked forward to the power, energy and knowledge IT would soon absorb and two more creatures would cease to exist upon the Earth.

Chapter 18

As Mariana approached her usual lunch spot, she saw a figure sitting on the rock where she generally perched. Incredibly, she recognized the man as Dr. Nezhoni! As she pulled up next to him, she saw that the inquisitive hawk she had been talking to over the past few weeks was perched on the rock next to Morgan.

She looked at him, noting that he didn't look surprised to see her. He looked a little rough around the edges and she observed the tree crutch next to him and the leather wrapped leg with stiff strips of wood extending from his foot to his knee. Getting out of her jeep, she took her lunch and an extra bottle of water with her.

When she sat down beside the man, the hawk looked at her, then back at Morgan. "It's okay Ona, you can go tell Ailiya that I am safe." With that, the hawk screeched and then took off with one powerful sweep of his wings.

She held out her hand. "Dr. Nezhoni, I am Mariana Thomas. Where have you been?"

He shook her hand and said, "Please, call me Morgan. Ailiya said you had been coming here every day the past few weeks. She thinks you are the person who saw her in your camera." He gratefully accepted the water bottle she held out to him in stunned disbelief.

"She's real?" Mariana asked incredulously.

With a wry grin, Morgan replied, "Yes, she is very much real. Believe me, it was quite a shock to me as well. But it is due to her that I am alive and well on the way to recovery." He motioned to his bound leg. "I tripped at the bottom of the canyon, breaking my leg. If she hadn't come to rescue me, I don't know what would have happened."

Mariana sat there, trying to absorb all that Morgan was telling her. She absently split her sandwich and offered him half as well as the container of fruit she had brought. She listened to Morgan describe who the creature was, she shook her head, no, who Ailiya was. She had a name and she was real!

* * *

Morgan laughed as Mariana overwhelmed him with questions. Her eyes were sparkling with excitement and the energy she exuded was palpable. Ailiya had recounted the impressions that Ona had of this young woman as she talked to him during her daily lunch breaks. Ona had understood much more than Mariana could have ever conceived.

Once Ailiya had determined that Morgan's leg and ankle had healed sufficiently, she had wrapped his leg a final time and given him a bag of herbs to decrease any discomfort he might still have and to aid in the continued healing. Gathering up his belongings and several gifts she had given him, she carried him to the top of the cliff, where the woman had been coming every day. She felt sadness at letting Morgan return to his world. It had been a long time since she had had a companion. At this thought, Ona had shrieked indignantly. "You are right Ona," she said out loud so that Morgan could understand why Ona was complaining. "I was thinking that it had been a long time since I had a companion and Ona just reminded me that he has been with me for a long time."

Ailiya looked sadly down at that ground. She had enjoyed having Morgan around and being able to talk to one of the people. She made sure that Ona knew she was talking about the people of the land. It had been so many years since Doba had returned to the Earth.

Morgan looked at her. "Ailiya, it is okay. I will return. Now that I know you are here, I will make sure you are protected. There is still so much that I don't know and so many questions that I have to ask of you!" She looked up shyly, smiling at Morgan.

Ailiya heard the sound of Mariana's vehicle approaching. She touched Morgan's amulet, warmth spread through him. "I am just a thought away," she said. With that, she told Ona to wait to make sure that Mariana took care of Morgan and she left to return to her cave.

* * *

Gotcha! Web had been working on the topographical map. He had Umberto move some of the cameras to focus in on the Frye Canyon area and on her known gardens and orchards. By doing this, he captured more day footage, but none led him directly to her cave or shelter.

The footage also showed that the creature was definitely a 'her'. While not mature or at least she hadn't born young, all of the video collaborated what the footprints had shown. Only one creature lived in the area.

He calculated the amount of food she would need, from the research he had already completed. He added an additional 50% for drying and storing for the winter and he had the information to show the creature collected and used a wide variety of foods daily. As certain plants bloomed, he saw she wouldn't collect all of one area, leaving older and younger plants each time she harvested. In reviewing information from those who 'wildcrafted' and from native cultures, he found that they generally left the oldest and youngest plants in order to perpetuate the planting and to help the young plants mature.

To Dale, this insight was significant. To him, it indicated a sentient creature, one that could communicate and plan. He continued trying to encourage Web to capture the creature, but he knew that nothing could deter Web once he had set upon a course. It was what made him a brilliant mercenary, one who had worked against his forces at times. As Web fed him information, he organized it into book fashion. If nothing else, perhaps he could write about the creature and what they learned. Under a pseudonym of course. He didn't want any of his old 'buddies' knowing that he believed in Sasquatch. If Web killed the creature, then they would have the video and the stills that Umberto had taken.

Chapter 19

Mariana gathered up the remains of their impromptu picnic, putting the remains in her bag and placing Morgan's belongings into the back seat of her jeep. She then helped Morgan to his feet, surprised at the warmth and strength she felt emanating from him. As he stood up, a stone talisman that he was wearing swung over, brushing against her cheek. Startled at the slight shock and the warmth which spread out of from where the stone had touched her face, she almost let go.

She looked at his leather cast. Morgan followed her gaze as he balanced himself with the crutch. "Ailiya rebound it this morning, making a special walking cast for me." he explained. Using the padded crutch Ailiya had made for him and with Mariana's help, he slowly made his way to the jeep, cautiously climbing inside, moving the seat back as far as he could before swinging his legs into the vehicle. "Thanks." he said, looking up into those brilliant eyes which seemed to be taking in every aspect of him.

Mariana blushed, realizing that she had been staring at him. He was quite attractive and given that she had spent a good part of the time of the last few weeks researching the man, she was a little disconcerted with the reality of actually finding him. She made sure he was comfortably seated and then jumped in on the driver's side.

"I have your belongings," she said. Glancing at him and seeing his surprised look she added, "The sheriff's department had the jeep returned to the rental agency and I picked up your luggage from the hotel. I hope you don't mind. I told one of the investigators that the newspaper was planning on running a story on you before your disappearance." again, she paused and blushed. She focused on avoiding the worst of the ruts after seeing the fleeting grimaces on Morgan's face. "After learning more about you, it wasn't that much of a white lie. I would like to do a story on you." As Morgan started to protest, she added, "Not about Ailiya. About your education at NAU and the places where you have been; especially the times when you have gone into catastrophe zones to help rescuers assess building stability."

"I do have lots of questions about Ailiya and what you have been through, but the newspaper editor and I have already buried the story behind the photo I took." At this, Morgan relaxed and waited for Mariana to negotiate the dirt road running along the edge of Frye canyon. Mariana had been up and down the road so many times in the past few weeks that she knew where most of the deep ruts and boulders in the roadway were. Once they hit 89A, going north to Flagstaff, Morgan was able to relax even further.

He looked at Mariana, who was intently thinking, absently chewing on her lower lip. She glanced at him, "I think we should take you to the Sheriff's department first. That way you can tell them that some good Samaritans took care of you. Then we can write a short article stating that you had been found. Is that okay with you?" He smiled, thinking that this one was beautiful and smart, always a deadly combination to him. He nodded. "Do we need to go to the hospital for your leg?" she asked him.

"No. Ailiya said the bones have already almost completely healed. She recommended that I keep the brace on for at least another week, primarily because of the sprain in my ankle." Morgan held up the small bag he had retained. "She gave me enough herbs to treat any discomfort and also packed a different mixture to soak my foot in once I remove the brace."

Mariana nodded again. "I am going to take you to my place where Frank and Amy can come meet you, if that is okay?" She waited for Morgan to reply and then explained that Frank was the editor for the Arizona Daily sun and Amy was his wife. She explained the research they had done as well as the removal of the evidence of Ailiya's flight through the forest in case someone else had glimpsed her at the edge of the construction site. "We don't think anyone else saw her, if they have, they haven't made it known."

* * *

Morgan relaxed in the relative comfort of Mariana's small house. It was actually a small carriage house that had been converted into a one bedroom house with a study. He had satisfied the police he didn't know who had taken care of him, just that they had cared for him until he was able to move around on his own.

Mariana had then hustled him away when it seemed like they were going to continue the questioning, particularly wondering how she was the one who had discovered him. She mentioned that they needed to get him off of his leg and get it elevated. He actually agreed with her, he was still worn out from all of the exertion and excitement of the day. Mariana assured the investigators the newspaper would include a blurb that Dr. Nezhoni had been found.

After she got him settled in the Murphy bed in the study of her home, she called Frank and then called Amy, telling them to bring food and to get to the house as soon as possible. She checked to see if Morgan wanted anything in particular, gave him some juice to mix in the herbs Ailiya had sent with him and quietly shut the door.

As he rested on the bed, with his leg duly

elevated as Mariana had informed the investigators was needed, he glanced about the small room. There was lots of artwork on the walls. He imagined they had been made by Amy, Mariana's friend. On the desk next to the fold down Murphy bed were several binders, full of printouts. Each binder was labeled. One was labeled with his name. Curious, he picked it up, to see what information Mariana had put together on him.

He smiled at the list of questions that was inserted in the clear sleeve of the front cover. It showed more about the way Mariana's mind worked. Thumbing through the binder, he was surprised at the amount and quality of the information Mariane had been able to gather on him. Having no real home of his own, he had never put down roots, except for the hogan behind his Aunt's place. He returned there when he could. He had a room in the house his parents owned in Tucson, but they were out of it as often as he was. It was simply a place to have their mail sent. He smiled at some of the questions Mariana had posed. Who is Morgan Nezhoni? How was he raised? Was his family traditional or respectful of the ways of their people? Is he connected? The last question was underlined and written with several question marks.

* * *

Ailiya watched from the trees across the canyon as Mariana helped Morgan into her jeep. Ona chirped at her, rubbing his beak in her fur, knowing that she felt sadness. She reached up and smoothed his feathers, reassuring him that she was okay; just wistful. She hadn't realized how lonely her existence had become until Morgan had entered her life again.

After she watched the jeep carefully pull away, she climbed down the tree and picked up the baskets that had been used in transporting the gifts and belongings of Morgan. She didn't want to go back to the emptiness of her cave. She turned off on one of the side canyons, to go tend one of her gardens. It was one in which very few hikers ever went to and she felt secure in that it was safe to be out in the daylight.

As she tended the garden and harvested the plants which were ripe, she started pondering what she was to do with her life. Now that Morgan knew of her existence, she would have periodic visits with him, but she was still essentially alone. She thought of the books and the history which her mother had buried in the desert. Thaena had told her that she would know when the time was right for her to retrieve the stone box. Searching her mind for the memories transferred at her mother's death, she did not feel that it was time. She would make sure to create a map and notes for Morgan, just in case something was to happen to her before she retrieved the information.

Morgan had told her of the Pacific Northwest, where there was always stories of Big Foot or Sasquatch. She remembered her mother telling her that many of the Elders of their kind made their homes in that land. Thaena had told her of the oceans, rivers and the great amount of rain the area received. Ailiya had liked the ocean. She remembered her swim with the dolphins and the stories and pictures they had given to her. She had drawn some of those images as her skills had increased. She liked the monsoon season in the canyon. Great booms of thunder would rumble through the canyons, followed by torrential rains. She sometimes would go out in the rain to run as most of the people of the Earth took shelter. Since she could feel the energy around her, she knew when the electrical buildup would result in lightning and she would be able to avoid those areas.

She shook her head. That still didn't solve her problem of being alone. The men that lived in the forest at the top of the canyons would get her supplies if she asked. She didn't think they really knew who or what she was. She provided foods or medicines if they left the flag up on their box. She had an ongoing chess game with one of them. Each time a move was made or a note would be left, the colored flag would be raised. When she had made her move and had left either supplies or requests for materials with jewelry or other items they could sell, she would raise the white flag. She made sure not to travel to the site except for at night or during storms.

Wearing her talisman now, she could feel a thread moving away from her, that would be Morgan's talisman as the dark haired woman drove him back to Flagstaff. Ona chirped again, he had liked the dark haired woman. She talked to him like Morgan did, not like an animal or a creature who couldn't understand her. He didn't understand everything she said to him, but she looked at him and asked questions as though he could answer her. Ailiya laughed, "See, you are going to miss them, too!" Ona gave a sad, short chirp, his way of agreeing with her and burrowed his head beneath the longer hair found at the back of Ailiya's head and neck.

Concentrating now on the talisman, she held it in one of her hands. Closing her eyes, she focused on the energy she felt emanating like threads away from her. She was surprised to find a very light one at a distance not too far from her. It felt familiar. Her fingers ran over the broken piece of the stone. It caused a tingling sensation which was very unpleasant to her. She thought it might be the broken piece of the talisman. If it was, then it was most likely in the possession of that horrid boy. She shuddered. If that was the case, she didn't like the way the grown man felt. The energy was malevolent, although there was a certain amount of excitement about it which hadn't existed the last time she had searched. Moving away from that path, she sensed the darker, even more evil thread. It was much closer than it had been before. She instinctively moved away from that thread as well.

Finally, she sought the bright, golden thread, which was also much, much closer than it had been before. It wasn't unpleasant, as the other two felt, but there was some kind of warning that she didn't quite understand. It felt more like a caution, like she was being warned to be careful. She didn't want to leave that connection, but Ona pecked her ear to get her attention. Startled, she let go of the talisman, abruptly pulling out of the slight trance she had been in. Feeling slightly disoriented, she asked Ona what was wrong. Ona was very agitated, there were things on some of the trees and there was a man on top of the canyon.

Ona took off from Ailiya's shoulder, flapping his great wings to get up to the level of the canyon. Seeing where the man was, he flew back down to Ailiya and told her he was sitting there, looking through 'long eyes', binoculars, searching the canyon floor. At that, Ailiya went back the way they had come and went down a side canyon to reach her home. She was disconcerted by this revelation. It would seem to be related to the broken piece of her own talisman. She was being hunted!

* * *

"Web?" Dale contacted Web through their secure connection. "You've got a big problem on your hands. Turn to the local newspaper website and then CNN." With that, he disconnected.

Web pulled up the website for the Arizona Daily Sun, the local newspaper in Flagstaff. Looking back at him was a grain, black and white photograph of the creature's face. "NO!" He screamed. "Umberto, come here this instant!"

When Umberto rushed into the room, it was to see Web in a rage that had never been matched before. He was throwing the plaster casts, upending the map table, anything he could reach was thrown. "Why did you do it?" raged Web. "Don't I pay you enough? Haven't I always taken care of you and your family?" All of this, while Umberto was ducking and dodging the flying plaster casts. He looked concerned at Web, whose flushed face and pulsing veins in both his neck and his temples indicated that he was in poor condition.

He shouted back at Web, in order to be heard over his rage. "What are you talking about? I have done nothing wrong!"

Web pointed to the computer monitor, which had so far escaped his torrent. "Look at that! Where did they get that picture at? How much did they pay you?" He continued to throw things and to pace back and forth from one end of the large room to the other.

Umberto edged his way closer to the monitor, so that he could look at the picture. "Senor, I do not know this picture. I did not take it and I would not turn against you. I know that all I have and all that my family has are because of you!" He ducked again as a container of push pins brushed past his shoulder. He crouched behind the antique wooden desk which housed the computer and monitor. He scrolled down to see the story. He read that a newspaper reporter had taken the photograph and written a story. He started reading it out loud to Web, giving him the name of Sid Rolfton as the writer. He had photographed the creature and sold the photograph to most of the more 'sensational' newspapers.

Umberto clicked on the CNN.com web link. It showed news stories featuring the controversial 'sighting' of the Sasquatch in the Flagstaff area. Most news reports were taking it as a hoax, but more and more encounters with the creature were being reported. However, the only photograph was the one shown on the front of the Daily Sun. There were no notes of plaster casts of footprints or hair samples. Supposed Sasquatch experts had been contacted and the overall perception was that the relative dryness of the area would make it undesirable for the species.

Web was calming down, using his great mental recollection to realize that they did not have a photograph showing her looking at the camera; all of their photographs were from the side or back. Even the ones that were taken from the front either showed the creature looking away from the camera, not directly at the camera. The quality was grainier as well. Web had the highest quality cameras installed. This picture appeared to be a large blow up taken from a hand held camera instead of from one mounted on a tripod or on a tree as theirs were.

Thinking harder, he knew that Umberto wouldn't betray him, knowing that he would pay with his life if he had. Without another word, he walked out of the ranch house, jumped into the jeep and took off in search of some way to salvage this disaster. With this newscast and report, he knew that the area would soon be crawling with amateurs and hunters. He needed to call in some favors and see if he could diffuse the situation, possibly by having someone confess to either creating the photograph or to creating a Sasquatch sighting as a practical joke.

Umberto, still shaking, started picking up the

map room and restoring order. He jumped when the secure phone rang. He saw on the computer that it was Dale Walters. He had heard Web talk about his old friend with great respect. Tentatively, he answered the connection. A kindly face looked at him, somewhat startled. Quickly, Dale recovered. "Umberto?" with the nod of Umberto's head, Dale continued. "Did Web leave?" Again, another nod. "Okay. We don't have much time. Get a pen and a piece of paper. Write down this number, my name and the following information." Umberto did as he was asked.

The information included a bank account number with contact information. Dale told him that this money was for him if something were to happen to Web. Dale was concerned with the extreme obsession which was manifesting itself in his old friend. He went on to tell Umberto where he lived and how to contact him in case things got out of hand.

Umberto wrote down all of the information and carefully placed the information in an inside pocket of his wallet. Technically, he was in the country illegally and he carried no identification, leaving that to Web. He asked Dale, "Why are you doing this? I thought you were Senor Web's friend?"

Dale gazed at the younger man, sensing the deep loyalty of the man who had traveled the world, helping and watching over Web. He drew a deep breath and went on, "I am concerned that this is one hunt that should not be completed. I always believed Web about the story that got him sent away to military school, but deep down, I thought he had just been confused and it had actually been a bear. I have been watching the footage you have shot and the photographs you have taken." Pausing, he saw Umberto swallow painfully and observed a hint of confusion in his eyes. "What I have seen is a wonderful creature that has done no harm to anyone. I heard back from some of the vet's who make their home in the forests around Flagstaff...I think you may have observed some of their camps?" Again, Umberto nodded. "All that I hear is of a being that has saved many lives and helps, not only those in need, but also helps with the general health of the forest and the canyons. The areas where your tracking has shown that are most frequented by the being is shown to have suffered the least damage when forest fires have raged all around and a great variety of vegetation, greater than any other in the southwest, is found in the very same canyons."

He looked deeply at Umberto. Umberto felt as though the man were reading his soul. Again, Dale confided, "When the time comes, I want to capture the creature, not kill her." With this, Umberto nodded emphatically.

"Senor," he began, "My grandfather told me of

one such creature, a male, who saved his life and provided for our family. I have done as Senor Web has instructed me to do, but from all of the hours of watching this 'being'." He liked the sound of a "being" instead of a "creature" or "monster" as Web insisted on calling her, "I have seen nothing but kindness and goodness. I have spoken to some of those who make the woods their home. They tell me of a certain box, which has two flags inside it. When one of them is sick or injured, they write a note and hang one of the flags. When the flag is removed, they check the box and there is food or medicine with instructions. Sometimes, she hangs the flag and she puts a note with a list of items that she could use and she always includes a piece of jewelry, a woven blanket or other item for them to use in getting supplies for themselves and for her. Senor Dale, this is a very honorable being and I do not want to see her harmed."

At this, Dale nodded. "Son, you have my contact information. When the time comes, do what you can to save the being. Does he ever have you go into town?" Umberto nodded. Dale continued, "There will be a package for you at the old movie theatre in Sedona, do you know it?" Again Umberto nodded. "I will include a satellite phone for you with pre-programmed numbers, some cash and a rifle with tranquilizer shots. If you are unable to stop Web, you must shoot him with the tranquilizer before he can kill the being, is that understood?"

Umberto nodded and indicated that he understood. Dale then told him how to delete their conversation history from the secure system. "Good man. Do your best and learn as much as you can. Do not mention this conversation and keep your head down." At this, Dale ended the connection and Umberto followed his instructions to verify that all trace of the communication was removed. He also scribbled on the next few pages of the notepad he had used, then burned those pages and the next 5 or so. He continued straightening up the room as he knew Web would be furious if the room was not as it had been prior to his rant.

Chapter 20

"FRANK! FRANK! WAKE UP!" Mariana had hustled Morgan into her jeep and rushed over to Frank and Amy's house when she had picked up her morning newspaper. Staring up at her was the grainy image she had taken of Ailiya. She couldn't believe it. She read through the title and then the byline under Sid Rolfton...that little weasel she thought to herself. He had never liked her and had never liked that Frank had hired her as a writer instead of just allowing her to freelance when she first moved to Flagstaff.

She thought back, wondering how he would have been able to get a copy of the image. She had made sure that no files had been copied to the network or even to her work computer. She remembered printing them and passing Sid in the hall as she rushed them back to Frank's office. He had been acting particularly nasty towards her since she was out of the office more. He was a good investigative reporter, but he generally lacked the tact needed in order to work well with others.

"FRANK!!!" With this, Amy opened the door before Mariana could pound on the door again. Morgan limped up behind her, as she had run to the front door the minute the jeep had slammed to a stop. Mariana held up the paper, showing Ailiya's image, "LOOK! Amy, what are we going to do?"

"Do about what?" Frank walked up behind his wife, wrapping his arms around her waist before seeing the picture on the front page of the newspaper. Shocked, he reached and pulled it away from Mariana. "How did this happen? I set the main article myself last night; it was about the possible school closures of one of the high schools. Sid??? How would he get this picture?" He turned and walked inside, waving at Mariana and Morgan to follow him to the kitchen table.

Amy held back, letting Mariana rush past her. She closed the door behind Morgan, asking if he needed any help. He shook his head. Amy directed him to the kitchen where they found Frank on the phone, angrily demanding of the production crew why the front page story was changed from what he submitted the night before. Amy held a chair for Morgan and asked if they had eaten anything. Morgan shook his head, looking very downcast. Amy moved over to the oven and added more eggs and bacon to what she already had cooking.

Mariana was on her cell phone, talking to their IT department to find out how a picture could have been saved in the system if it hadn't been saved on the computers. She learned that the print server could be accessed at a later date to print the project again. She sighed...that was how Sid had managed to get a copy of her picture. He must have realized that something was up and had gone into the print server history and printed out the last copy of photos that she had printed. She remembered passing him after picking up the photos before taking them to Frank.

* * *

When Web returned, his coloring was almost normal and the veins weren't throbbing in his head anymore. He was able to think with clarity and to ponder his next moves. He had called on several friends to 'debunk' and 'demystify' the supposed Sasquatch sighting. Surprising, when he reached Sedona and picked up the Daily Sun, he saw that a retraction had been posted with regard to the photo. The article noted that the photo had been put together and posted by a disgruntled employee who had lost his job. Web was perplexed by this. It meant that someone out there knew of the creature and they were doing their best to keep it quiet. His guys hadn't had time yet to dispel the story, but he knew that the fire was already well on its way to being put out.

He knew that he would have to lay low for awhile, until any curiosity seekers had grown weary and left the area. Come, they would, he knew. From his past research, whenever there was a supposed sighting, hordes of people and hunters alike would pour into the area, searching for any sign of the creature.

Once back at the ranch house, he told Umberto to go remove the cameras, except for the few that focused in at Frye Canyon. These, he was to ensure were completely camouflaged and to install more powerful batteries so he could remove the reflective solar power panels. With relief, Umberto quickly packed the gear he needed and left. He was still mulling over Web's reaction and the information he had been given by Dale. He knew he would have to be careful as Web would be even more paranoid and suspicious. Although he loved the man, almost as a father, he had paid a great price in the service of Web. He knew the next generation of his family was secure, having put his nieces and nephews through college so that they would not have to suffer the hunger and fear that he and his siblings had once faced. But he had done many things that he was not proud of. He did not have the soul of a good mercenary. He still believed in a right or wrong way of life. When Web's father passed and Web turned his attention to hunting, Umberto had heaved a great sigh of relief. He was much more comfortable with poaching or even with hunting endangered animals than he had ever been with helping Web hunt men.

While in the canyon, he spotted the box Dale had told him about. After making sure that none of the cameras were positioned so they could see the box, he went to the box, put up both flags and wrote a note on the notepad he found in there.

To the being who lives in this canyon: Please know that there is danger for you and for those who help you.

He didn't sign it and was very careful to use a different type of printing in case Web heard of this location and found the note. He couldn't do anymore for those who helped the being or for the being herself. He gathered up his tools and started back to the ranch house.

Chapter 21

Umberto used the excuse of needing some fresh supplies in order to go into town. Web gave him a list of additional supplies he needed. When reaching town, Umberto went to the theatre. The package had been left where Dale had indicated, with further information for Umberto.

Picking up the latest newspapers, he saw that the furor over the Sasquatch sighting had not completely died off. Web's people and whoever had been helping the being, had done well in taking the story out of the mainstream. However, the being's face was still being shown on all of the newspaper tabloids with wild stories of "Sasquatch Invasion", "Monster Abductions" and of course the ever popular "I was Impregnated by Sasquatch". He laughed, but gathered them up and purchased them anyway, knowing that Web would want any and all information.

It took him awhile to obtain all of the materials and supplies Web wanted. He had to go all of the way into Cottonwood to purchase some of the goods. Sedona was more of a town for tourists, there were some grocery stores and hardware stores, but not a lot of variety. Cottonwood was the closest town that had larger stores and supplies.

On his way back to the ranch, he started feeling like something was wrong. He took the package

Dale had sent, and made sure the tranquilizer gun was loaded and that he understood how to use it. He pulled into the ranch to find that all was silent. He unpacked the supplies, with a sense of unease. He had the only vehicle; there were no pack animals on the ranch.

He finished unloading and sorting through the mail that had been forwarded to Sedona. He placed it on the desk in the map room. As he did, he bumped the mouse so that the screen saver stopped and he saw Dale, waiting impatiently on the video screen. "Umberto!" Dale cried. "You must hurry! Web felt that the creature left the canyon and has gone in search of her. He was also mumbling something about being in a race with another creature. He left without shutting off our connection, so I've been waiting for you to get back to the ranch."

Umberto looked concerned. "Where do I go? If the being has left the canyon, I don't know where to look. Web had me take down all of the outlying cameras. Wait!" He paused excitedly; he turned the screen containing the image of Dale and the video camera towards the map table. He moved to the table, looking at the only place on the map where Web had gone to place a camera. He noted the number and pulled up the camera on the screen. It showed a red rock canyon and a dry stream bed. Looking closely, he could see a dark shadow sitting on an elevated flat slab. Using the automated controls, he was able to zoom in and see that it was the being, sitting cross-legged on the slab with her palms flat on the sun warmed sandstone. He uploaded the link to Dale and went back to the map.

"This is the location where the being's mother had been killed and where Web had been scared." Umberto said over his shoulder to the monitor. "There are no easy ways to get to this location." He pondered the easiest way to reach the spot. "Why would he go there now?" He asked Dale. "We never saw any footage of the being visiting this area. When Web had me remove and reposition the cameras, he insisted that this one stay where it is."

Dale spoke up, "He said that the stone from the mother's talisman felt like it was on fire. He also said that he had been able to feel three strong emanations from the stone and that they were all going to meet up today, at that spot." He was quickly thinking of how he could get extra help. "Umberto, get there as fast as you can. Did you get my package?" Umberto nodded as he started gather maps, equipment and supplies, the camera automatically following him as he moved about the room. "Good. You better take a regular pistol or rifle as well, in case there are problems. Leave the connection running. Good luck." He called the last out as he saw Umberto run for the door.

Turning, Dale called the Daily Sun and asked to speak with the Editor-in-Chief.

* * *

IT could feel two of the creatures. They were in relatively close proximity to each other. IT didn't know if they knew of each other. IT knew that there weren't a lot of creatures left upon the face of the Earth. Of the ones that were left, very few connected to each other through the energies of the Earth. There were a few creatures though that was different. They had ways of blocking IT from knowing where they were.

When IT was in stasis, these minor connections were not strong enough to rouse IT. Now that IT was moving through the Earth, the connections seemed to be blips from around the world. Small clusters would be felt and ignored, IT knew where the lost creature had been and that was where IT was heading. From that location and unshielded, as the others blips were, IT was flowing faster through the Earth's energies, towards the target.

IT remembered being formed, receiving knowledge, but not life. Loathing turned to hatred, hatred fueling evil. At first, many creatures roamed throughout the Earth, even as the Earth changed, they moved. Like IT, they could feel the rumblings of the huge plates making up the continents of the Earth. The rise and fall of the oceans, the rise and fall of the temperature, changing the environment, the continents and the very makeup of the surface of the world.

IT loved sliding through the overlapping plates, almost playing with the heated rock, hitting a thermal pocket and shooting out of what was called a volcano. The changing magnetic fields of the Earth along with the inherent energies allowed IT to explore all corners of the Earth, above and below the crust. IT couldn't go much deeper than the molten outer layer. When going too deep IT found that IT lost mass, matter, energy and strength. IT long ago learned to love the heat near the surface as well as the cool, dark places, such as the cave where IT had recently been roused. IT had several favorite locations where IT would go back to after absorbing the hated creatures. In the cool depths of the caves, IT would sort through the energy and knowledge which IT had gained.

Chapter 22

It would be today! Web was ecstatic. The excitement made him feel lightheaded. He had a rough night; horrible nightmares of that day long ago kept creeping into his dreams. He had felt clammy and sweaty for the last few days as well. He attributed that to the heat that seemed to emanate from his ring. He could definitely feel the pull of three separate entities now. For the longest time, the two had remained close together, likely in Frye Canyon where the creature appeared to hole up. The other pull that had been from the south was close now, so close that Web almost felt like he could feel the creature breathing down his neck.

He had given Umberto a long list of supplies, knowing that his assistant would have to travel to Cottonwood in search of some of the items. Although as close to a son as he would ever have, he didn't trust Umberto anymore. At least, not about this hunt. Umberto had stayed by his side through some of the nastiest fighting and assassinations they had been tasked to accomplish, but for some reason, he felt as if Umberto's heart was not in this hunt.

After Umberto left, he packed up his supplies and loaded his weapons. He would take no chance with this hunt. He took a 4x4 out of the back of the barn. Not even Umberto knew it was there. He piled on additional fuel, water, ammunition and other items to help him with the hunt. He felt almost feverish now. He was beginning to tremble and drop items. He blamed it on not eating and on the heat from the ring causing his hands to be sweaty.

Finally, after he had everything ready, he took off down the jeep road, cutting through a few back trails in order to reach the base of the canyon. He didn't question his actions; he knew that the abominable beast would be at the same place where her mother had died on that fateful morning. For the first time, he stopped in his thinking to wonder what had killed the mother. He hadn't hit her and the stone hadn't hit her that hard. Thinking back, he remembered that the creature had reared back, right before he had let loose with his slingshot. He finally started wondering why the stone in his ring behaved so differently. It was almost like a force field around him now. While he knew that the small piece was letting him know of the creature's location, he wondered if it worked the other way as well. Could she know that he was on his way to kill her?

* * *

"Ailiya" a soft voice echoed through her head. Again, "Ailiya...come to me". It awoke her from her daydreams. She couldn't see anyone and the voice didn't sound like anyone she knew. Fully aware now, the voice softly whispered, "Ailiya...come to me. Come talk to me. You miss me. You need me. Ailiya...come to me."

Shaking her head as if clearing it from a fog, an image was placed in her mind of the canyon where her mother had long ago used to travel to in order to connect to the Earth. Could it be her mother? It didn't sound like her mother. Her mother was dead...it couldn't be her. Ailiya focused deeper. She still couldn't tell who it was.

Missing Morgan and Mariana and feeling slightly sorry for herself, she cleaned up her cave, in preparation of leaving for the canyon site. The voice kept repeating in her head. But something wasn't right. She didn't know what it was, but there was something wrong with the voice. It was oily, yet like two rocks grating against each other. It sounded old, older than anything she knew of.

At the same time, there wasn't a voice, but a feeling that kept coming to her. It seemed to tell her to be patient, to wait. She didn't want to wait anymore! She had been waiting for too many seasons.

Chapter 23

Finally, Web had left the 4x4 back down the dry wash and hiked the last few miles up to the familiar countryside that was revisited in his nightmares so many times in the past. As he approached the bend in the river bank, he again heard a deep humming, making the hairs on his arm stand up. He stopped to calm his heart rate and to settle his nerves. He had left the ring with his piece of the talisman back at the 4x4, not wanting to give away his position if it was somehow transmitting back to the other links.

Shaking, he pulled out his water bottle, drank some of the water, hoping that it would cool his overheated body. He thought that when he took the ring off that the feverish condition would go away. He felt as if it had gotten worse once he removed it. Sweating, he removed his hat and wiped his arm across brow and then dried his hands on his pants.

Carefully, he put his pack on the ground and began to assemble his rifle and high powered scope. This done, he again drank more water, wondering if in his haste he was getting heatstroke by being out in the sun so long and was dehydrated. He was dressed in a red stone colored camouflage he had made to order. Even his hat was made to blend into the range of colors around him. He threw the special made cover over his rifle and made sure that he could look unimpeded through the scope.

He had long ago chosen his spot, if this canyon was going to be his kill zone. By going around the other side of the large boulder at the bend in the wash, soft sand had been deposited almost directly across from the creature's perch. He saw dots swimming in front of his eyes now. He drank more water, but felt nauseous.

Slowly, he climbed up the hill of sand, carefully peeking around the corner. There! On the perch, just as her mother had been was the creature that had roared at him through countless nightmares. She was in a meditation pose and the humming sound increased as he settled himself below the top of the hill. By now, he had goose bumps and the hair on the back of his neck was prickling.

The creature's eyes were closed. He noted the beautiful, silky hair of her pelt, thinking to himself that it would make a wonderful blanket that he would sleep with every night. He kept blinking to remove the sweat that was dripping in his face, but with no luck. He removed the screened hat so that he could wipe his forehead.

This done, he steadied his rifle on the top of the sand hill. Looking through the scope, he found that he was still shaking too much. Closing his eyes, he breathed deep, trying to steady his heart rate. He was so excited; it almost felt as if his heart was going to break through his chest.

Pausing now to look at the scope, he found he was much steadier and he was able to retreat into the actions that had kept him alive throughout countless wars and military actions. The buzzing of the insects, the strange humming that was emanating from the very sandstone walls around him, even the screech of a bird of prey, these were pushed to the back of his mind. As he breathed out, he tightened his finger on the trigger.

* * *

Finally! IT thought in exultation. IT could feel the creature in her trance. Her connection was the deepest one yet as it almost flew through the mineral and energy lines surrounding her. IT wasn't concerned that both of the creatures weren't connected. Once IT absorbed the female creature, the male would be next.

The power of the creature's connection, as well as the strength of the bond with the unique geology of the region entranced IT. Through small tendrils, IT began penetrating the red, iron rich stone on which the creature had seated herself. The tendrils wound up clumps of the creature's fur. IT was in no hurry, now that the destination had finally been reached, and to savor the experience meant to draw out the absorbing of the creature's essence and knowledge.

Remembering IT's last great absorbing of the creatures helped IT to make sure the creature was solidly connected and fully in her trance before the tendrils round around her fur, tracing lines lightly across her skin which was in contact with stone.

IT could feel another creature closing in on their location. IT also sensed several men in the area. The men did not bother IT. IT was not able to contact or absorb man. Animals and the hated creature it was slowly wending IT's way around, were all that IT was allowed.

The creature still didn't know it was in IT's grasp. IT savored the energy reverberating around them; it had been such a long time since IT had felt the knowledge transfer that was beginning to occur.

Still holding off, savoring the energy and knowledge, IT was biding time, not knowing for what IT waited. Finally, when IT could withstand no more, it allowed the tendrils to begin absorbing the creature. Such knowledge! Such power! The creature was not even aware of how much knowledge and potential that she had. But IT knew. IT knew! Exultation filled IT and blocked out all awareness except for the absorption of the creature and of the resistance it was fighting with.

Chapter 24

Ona screeched again, flying near to Ailiya. She didn't appear to hear him. She didn't budge from her trance on the stone. Suddenly, Ailiya screamed, Ona felt great pain washing through Ailiya.

Ona felt it was from the man, hiding behind the boulder. Again, he screeched at Ailiya, who was writhing in pain on the ledge. This time, Ona placed himself directly between the strange man with the gun and his own Ailiya. Using his powerful wings, Ona flew straight at the man, just as the gun bellowed.

"NO!" Web screamed, jumping up from his hiding place in rage. The bird fell to the ground; it had deflected the power of the bullet so that instead of tearing into the creature's heart, it hit the cliffs above her, knocking loose rocks that rained down onto the creature. He watched as the creature began to tumble from the perch.

He heard distant voices screaming, "Stop, don't shoot!" Startled, he automatically drew down and shot at the figures running towards him.

At the same time, he felt a sharp pain in his back and then a crushing blow as a huge weight landed on him. The weight soon left him, but he couldn't move. He saw a large, dark creature bound in front of him, to go to aid of the hated creature. Something else, a heaviness to his heart, it seemed to take forever for it to pump. He couldn't breathe. The creature was down, but the humming in the canyon didn't cease. Suddenly, he heard Umberto calling to him and then a great, black burning engulfed him. His last thoughts were that he had failed once again.

* * *

"NO!" Brozan screamed as he searched his memory for any way to combat the creature that was engulfing Ailiya. He had heard her scream and as he raced around the bend in the stone canyon, he saw her arch her back and scream again. His thoughts raced. He had never felt such power of the Earth as he did in this unique geologic area.

Spying the man aiming the gun at other humans, who were yelling at the man and for Ailiya, he made a giant leap, knocking the man onto his stomach. Kneeling on the man, he immediately became aware of several problems. Regardless, he shook his head; he felt the man's utter hatred of Ailiya. He knew that the man would never stop in his search of their kind, not just of Ailiya.

Looking up, he saw that Ailiya was falling off of the stone ledge, the dark substance that was entangled in her fur was stretching, but was maintaining its connection to both the stone and to

Ailiya. Centering himself, he reached out, gathering all of the power from the surrounding stone. Both magnetic and energy levels of the Earth met in this canyon, "No wonder Thaena was able to reach around the world." he thought, "Never have I felt such power."

Using this strength and knowing that the creature feasted upon the power, Brozan reached out, grasping the essence of the creature, yanking it out of the stone and from around Ailiya. He could feel the hatred of the creature and its surprise as it was literally ripped out of the energy fields. He paused, waiting. At the last moment, he jumped, up and forward, towards Ailiya.

The creature had quickly adjusted to being torn from the rock and its prey and focused in on the one other Elo-ai-ne who had escaped its grasp so many years ago. Gathering the energy around it, the creature soared towards Brozan, who suddenly wasn't there.

* * *

Suddenly, IT found itself ripped free of both the creature and from the stone where they had been entwined. Never had IT moved under the power of another. "NO!" IT screamed silently. IT was not to be denied again, not from this location and not from the daughter of the creature IT had once tried to absorb.

Without realizing what was happening, IT found itself flying towards the other creature. As tortured as IT felt when ripped from the female creature and the energies of the surrounding stone, some part felt exultation as IT realized that the male creature was the other creature who had escaped IT during the great explosion!

"NOOOOOO..." Confused, IT found itself devouring a man. The creature was gone. IT realized that the creature had been crouched over the man and that it was the power of the creature that had wrenched IT from both stone and creature.

As the man was dissolving, so was IT. Soon, there would be nothing. All of IT's knowledge, gained through the eons was gone in a flash. As IT's knowledge disappeared, IT's sense of self too was dissolving, till nothing remained except an energy resonance which soon faded.

Chapter 25

"Mariana!" Morgan cried, turning to see Mariana lying on the ground, with blood seeping down the side of her arm. "Are you ok?"

Dazed, Mariana realized that she was on the ground. She didn't remember tripping or falling. She followed Morgan's gaze to see blood oozing from a long tear in her sweater. She looked up at Morgan, not comprehending that she had just been shot.

Morgan dropped to his knees, tearing her sweater more, to see where she had been hit. With relief, he realized that although she had been hit twice, one appeared to be a thru and thru, at the fleshy part of her underarm/side area and the other had just grazed the outside of her arm, neither injury was life threatening.

Mariana looked at the wounds, then back at Morgan, saying, "It's just a flesh wound..." with a British accent reminiscent of the dialog from Monty Python and the Holy Grail. "...not dead yet. I want to go for a walk!"

Morgan laughed, stood up and then helped Mariana to stand. He scooped her up in his arms, with Mariana repeating "...but I'm not dead yet...I want to go for a walk!"

"Hush," Morgan says. "Let's get you back to the cave and get that cleaned up."

"No, seriously, I can walk..." Mariana managed weakly before she realized that shock and blood loss was setting in and she probably wouldn't be able to walk anyway. "Where is Ailiya and where is that creep that shot me?" She suddenly demanded, struggling in Morgan's arms.

They both turned to look and they saw another Elo-ai-ne leaning over Ailiya. It was bigger and larger than Ailiya. It looked up and in a deep voice demanded, "Show me her cave." Brozan picked up Ailiya and began following the couple in front of him. They led him to the base of the cliff, where Morgan put Mariana down and cleared the rocks and plants that Ailiya used to hide the trail.

Brozan carried Ailiya up the trail, pausing at the front of the cave, letting his eyes adjust. Seeing the pile of furs in the back, he took her there and gently placed her in the middle. He looked up as Morgan helped Mariana into the cave, placing her on the bed. "Start a fire." Brozan told Morgan.

Morgan went to the hearth and stirred up the coals, adding additional tinder and smaller pieces till the flames were roaring. He put a pot of water over the flames and another one with a soup preparation. He got out the herbs Ailiya had used on him and mixed a drink for Mariana as he waited for the water to boil.

Brozan sat at Ailiya's head, with his hands placed to either side of her face. He visually observed the burns from the dark creature as well as the crease in her skin at the top of her head caused by the grazing of the bullet that had passed through Ona. He searched for the life spark that was Ailiya, trying to fuel it as the man had done to the fire. He called to her spirit, asking her not to leave him, not when he had finally found her. Faintly, as though a candle seen from a distance, he sensed the softly glowing spark that is Ailiya. He couldn't communicate with her; it was as though she had curled up and wrapped a protective layer around what was left of her spirit. He sighed with relief though, knowing that she was still there. Keeping his hands on her face, he continued to gently feed her spirit with his energy.

Mariana continued to spout movie clips at Morgan, even more after he had given her the laced juice. Morgan couldn't believe her spirit, how well she had handled the violent confrontation they had been through. She gazed up dreamily at him when he carefully cut the sleeve of her sweater off and down her side. "You're cute! You know that...you are really cute." At that, she closed her eyes and slept. Morgan smiled...she was really growing on him. He cut the rest of the sleeve off of her arm, so that he didn't have to pull it over the wound. Her modesty would remain somewhat intact. The shot that grazed her side was above her bra strap and looked like it would just need butterfly band aids to close. The one that penetrated her arm was along the inner edge. It was thru and thru, all he could do was clean it out. His heart fluttered as he realized how lucky she had been.

Morgan went to where Ailiya had stored clean cloths. He removed the boiling water, taking it further back in the cave to where Brozan tended Ailiya. Brozan said, "Tend the woman first." nodding towards where Mariana lay on the bed. "Ailiya is not strong enough yet." With that, he turned his attention inward, feeding more energy to the bright spark that stayed tantalizingly out of his grasp.

Morgan returned to Mariana and used the water to saturate one of the cloths which he then used to remove the dried blood from Mariana's arm and her side. When he finished, he looked towards the male Elo-ai-ne who was caring for Ailiya. "Which herbs should I use?" He had either been in too much pain when Ailiya had cared for him or he had forgotten which of the multicolored herbs were for injuries. He had a tray filled with small baskets. Each basket contained a different herb. He carefully carried this tray back to Brozan.

Brozan looked at the herbs, "Use those two, mixed into a paste and then bind the wound." Morgan picked out the two baskets, verified he had the right two and did as Brozan had told him to do. After cleaning, he placed thick fabric bandages on the wounds, tying additional straps around her rib cage and around her arm, binding the bandages at both the entrance and exit wounds. The bullet had caused a lot of damage to the back of her arm and all he could do was bandage it tightly. He then covered Mariana with one of the woven blankets, brushing the hair from her eyes as she slept.

He put the water back over the flames, adding more water to the broth mix, knowing that both Mariana and Ailiya would need it when they recovered consciousness. He looked over at the Elo-ai-ne and said, "My name is Morgan. The woman is Mariana. We are friends of Ailiya." Brozan nodded, continuing his vigil to bring Ailiya back, saying only, "Brozan."

Once the water was again heated, he carried the pot and additional clothes to where Brozan sat cradling Ailiya. He brought over the container which stored a salve that Ailiya had used on his scrapes when he was in the cave. Brozan nodded and then asked Morgan to carefully wash away the burned hair and tissue on her legs, side and head. Morgan also wiped away the clotted blood from the bullet crease on her head. He looked up at Brozan and asked if she was truly still alive; he didn't see her breathe and hadn't felt a pulse. Brozan nodded and said, "Barely, but I must concentrate to convince her to come back to us." Morgan then applied the salve liberally to the burned patches of Ailiya's skin, trusting in Brozan.

Chapter 26

Umberto threw down the gun, running towards Web. He saw the dart hit Web squarely in the back and then saw a large creature land on top of Web. He heard voices yelling at Web to stop, coming from the other side of the bend.

Suddenly, he screamed in horror! Web was dissolving! Dropping to his knees, careful not to touch the black mass that had engulfed Web, he could only watch as even the gun and the clothing were dissolved until there was nothing left.

Looking up, he saw an even larger, darker creature than the being they had been tracking, pick her up and speak in English to the man and the woman who had raced around the corner. All four soon left, rushing up the canyon. The man was carrying the woman, who looked like she had been shot by Web and the dark creature was carrying the apparently lifeless being that Web had been hunting. But something else was wrong with her. She didn't appear to be shot, except for a crease at the top of her head. There was a foul stench in the air that was a combination of burned hair and skin along with another smell he couldn't identify.

Incredulously, he looked again to where Web had been. There was nothing left to indicate that the man, who had just disappeared, had even existed. He walked around the boulder, until he saw the partial remains of the hawk that had swooped towards Web and had actually saved the being's life. Gently, he picked it up and placed it upon the ledge where the being had been sitting.

Noise returned to the canyon, not the buzzing of the rocks that had so puzzled him, but the animals, birds and insects all seemed to start communicating at once. With one look back to the location where Web had been, Umberto picked up Web's pack and walked back to where he had seen the 4x4. In the seat were the keys and the ring Web had always worn. Umberto put the ring on; feeling comfort from the warmth it gave to him. He drove the 4x4 to the jeep and then transferred the supplies to the jeep. He left a note and the keys in the 4x4, leaving it to whoever found it.

Driving back to the ranch, he did so with a sense of urgency. He did not know why, but it was important that he pack up and leave. Once at the ranch, he packed up his belongings, some of Web's favorite collections from his world travels and the framed picture of John Wayne. Umberto shook his head. Web never did get the sentiment the great man was trying to teach him all those long years ago.

Going into the map room, he saw the connection to Dale was still open. Dale had watched the whole exchange from the camera Web had installed at the canyon, across from where he had chosen to shoot the creature. Dale looked at Umberto with compassion. He gave him directions and the combination to Web's wall safe so he could bring the needed papers with him and have the cash necessary to travel.

As the sun set, Umberto raced away from the ranch, knowing he would never set foot in that area again.

Chapter 27

It was sundown before Brozan let go of Ailiya. He looked over at Morgan who was taking care of Mariana. Morgan met his eyes as Brozan nodded at him and said that Ailiya was stable. He stood, his stretching arms touching the height of the cave.

He ate some of the food Morgan had prepared and drank some of the fruit juice. He told Morgan there was unfinished business he needed to take care of. Morgan looked at him questioningly, but received no answer.

Brozan left the shelter, looking up into the fading light of the setting sun. He breathed deeply, the air was fresh and clean. He had been so focused on strengthening Ailiya and convincing her to not leave him alone, that he had not noticed how closed the air in the cave had been. The air had been filled with the metallic taste of blood from both Ailiya's and Mariana's injuries. Scorched skin, pelt and hair also scented the air. He had almost lost Ailiya several times, but his strength was able to support her until she realized she was not ready to leave this Earth.

Pausing, Brozan felt tentatively through the energies around him, sensing the locations of the cameras Web had Umberto install. He set out, going to each location and destroying the cameras. He did understand the cameras were all sending a signal back to a central location.

After he had destroyed all of the cameras he sensed, he headed towards the central location where the signals had been transmitted. He could sense a strong energy from that location but could not tell which direction or where it was moving due to the magnetic interferences from the red stones around him. He found himself being led to a beautiful valley floor. A creek ran through the valley and was filled with various orchard trees, grasses and fruit bearing bushes. At the edge of the valley, next to the base of a cliff, stood a house. It was to this location the cameras had been sending their signal. Several cameras were still in operation around the structure. He went to each one, purposefully grabbing them and tearing them from the wired connections. He went into the structure and found the obsession that had haunted the man who had hunted Ailiya.

He smashed the table showing the topographical area where Ailiya's cave had been. He could still feel a strong energy transmission, especially now that he was not in direct contact to the red stones. He found a closet where the energy felt the strongest and opened the door. Startled he saw a high-definition image of himself looking back at him. He realized there was a camera in the closet and that it was connected to the equipment sending the images. He roared into his image on the video screen, grabbed the camera, and ripped it from the wall. He then scoured the property for additional power sources.

* * *

Ailiya slowly regained consciousness. She felt so confused, she didn't understand why she hurt or recognize the sounds around her. The moment she started to move, a familiar hand was placed on her head. It was Brozan! In a rush, the incidents surrounding her injuries flooded her mind. She started to cry, for herself, for her parents and for the little boy who had turned into a monster. Arms gathered her up, holding her, comforting her. She drifted back into a restless, pain filled sleep.

Once Brozan knew that Ailiya had returned to the safety and peace of sleep, he placed her carefully upon her sleeping pads. He had returned just moments earlier, exhausted mentally and physically from the destruction of the recording devices at Web's home. He did not know where it was being transmitted to. What worried him more was who was on the receiving end. In searching the structure, he had seen evidence that Umberto had quickly packed and fled the area. Once Ailiya was more stable, he would give the computer to Morgan to see if he could figure out where the signal had gone. He was aware of computers, but he did not know the extent of their knowledge or communication abilities.

Morgan had seen a small laptop carried by Brozan, but did not ask where he had obtained it. He could sense the utter exhaustion that lay heavily upon Brozan. Morgan had been busy preparing foods, caring for Ailiya's wounds as well as keeping Mariana comfortable. He had indeed mixed herbs which had reduced her pain and shock from the bullet wound, but she seemed to be having a lot of strange dreams. Later, Brozan told him that he had inadvertently mixed peyote into her drink.

Chapter 28

Anger pulsed through Brozan. He hadn't been able to block Ailiya from broadcasting. Her abilities had soared since her ordeal. She didn't realize what she was doing when she wasn't quite awake. She had awakened in pain, sending out signals far and near. He had immediately jumped to her side, gently placing his arms around her. Feeling his touch, she quieted and settled her head onto his chest. He helped her slip back into a deep, therapeutic sleep, hopefully dreamless and pain free as he set blocks in her system to reduce the pain.

Her skin was healing, but large patches were scarring, despite his care and there were areas on her legs, feet and backside where her pelt wasn't growing back. Once all of the trimmed hair grew out, they wouldn't be noticeable, but he had felt her embarrassment when she had awakened earlier.

He thought back to the end of the season feast. Morgan and Mariana along with Frank and Amy had brought gifts, foods and a medical air bed, extra large, for Ailiya. Tears had coursed down Ailiya's cheeks as they set up the bed and showed Brozan how to operate the pumps. Amy had made a caftan for Ailiya, out of a brilliantly patterned silk fabric.

* * *

"There, there." Amy said as she helped Ailiya fit it over her head. She placed her hand on Ailiya's tear dampened cheek and looked into her eyes. "I thought you might like something to help prevent chafing until your skin heals and your own beautiful hair grows back. This is natural silk and I dyed it using traditional plant dyes, so there shouldn't be anything to interfere in your healing." She grinned mischievously, "Morgan told us about your 'shampoo' incident in the pond. The owners of the house are old friends of mine; I remember them telling me about the odd suds they found one morning. They have also told me about weird howling sounds on moonless nights." With this, Amy burst into peals of laughter at the guilty expression on Ailiya's face. "Don't worry about it honey! You have been a part of this country longer than anyone else and your existence has added to the mystic and magic of our area!" At this, Amy asked to see Ailiya's art portfolio. They sat on the rock at the front of the cave and looked through the portfolio while the others arranged and prepared the food for the traditional feast before the winter sleep.

There were many native foods, as well as treats the humans wanted to share with the Elo-ai-ne. Brozan offered a traditional blessing for the bounty that was spread before them.

Ailiya had received gifts from all of them and she had prepared small drawings for each of them, some portrayed animals and others were scenes from the now deserted native buildings surrounding the San Francisco Peaks. She kept touching the art supplies Amy had brought her...beautiful hues of a soft chalk that Amy told her were called 'pastels'. She had also included pencils of various shades and a watercolor pencil set Amy told her would turn into soft, water shades when a wet brush was pulled across the lines. Ailiya had never felt such wonderful paper and Amy had given her several different sized pads and types of paper for her to experiment with.

It wasn't long before Ailiya tired and asked to try out her new bed. She was in pain and ready for a long sleep. As she reclined on her new bed, she marveled at the comfort and at the generosity of those surrounding her. She had been all alone for so long and now she had so many friends that her cave almost felt crowded.

She drifted in and out of sleep, aware that Brozan had liberally laced her fruit drink with powerful pain killing herbs and some others to help promote sleep. She didn't mind. She had fully enjoyed the celebration...it had been such a long time since she had had anyone to celebrate the end of the year festival.

She roused once all of the foods had been

cleaned up and their visitors were ready to leave. There were tears in everyone's eyes as they said their goodbyes for the season. Brozan had small pouches he gave to each of them. Ailiya didn't know what was in them, but he looked happy to be able to give gifts to those who had befriended her.

After they left, Brozan fitted the wood panels that blocked the cave entrance during the winter months. Ailiya had carefully carved them to resemble stone and had stained them to match the surrounding stones. She had even attached dried plants so that the area would completely blend away.

Ailiya was already drowsing by the time Brozan returned to his sleeping pad, placed near her new bed. She looked up gratefully at him and held out her hand to him. He sat on his sleeping furs, clasping her hand in both of his, feeling her slowing system react to the herbs he had given her. Ailiya smiled. "Thank you Brozan. Thank you for coming back for me and for saving my life. If you hadn't been here, I wouldn't have survived the entity."

At this, Brozan kissed her on top of her head, cupping her cheek with his hand. "Ailiya, I have searched for you for many seasons and through many continents. I, too, am thankful I was able to arrive when I did. However, you have had enough excitement and you need to fall into a long, deep sleep so you can heal."

Ailiya smiled, "Yes Brozan, I will rest now. Just one question, why did you come looking for me?"

"That, my dear," he smiled as Ailiya placed her hand on his, "is the promise I made to you when we were young."

* * *

She was alive! Bronan had sensed her in the moment it took his brother to block him. She was in pain and she was weak, but she was alive. He hadn't seen his brother in many seasons, since he had left to meet with the Elders in the northwest area of the continent.

Bronan sighed in satisfaction. His brother would bring her to him, he would have no option. He started making plans.

ABOUT THE AUTHOR

Born and raised in the Southwest, including a year in Kayenta on the Navajo Indian Reservation, the history, knowledge, and beauty of the area has always captured Valerie Farr's interest. A licensed Professional Engineer, photographer, and former reporter, she was able to combine both her analytic skills as well as her artistic skills in creating the world of the Elo-ai-ne and Ailiya. Her experiences with native Rock Art, the traditions of the various peoples who inhabited the Southwest, and a desire to share her experiences evolved into this story, which grew from the natural beauty around her.